I0788566

TRAFALGAR & BOONE AND THE CHILDREN OF THE BURNT EMPIRE

TRAFALGAR & BOONE BOOK FOUR

Geonn Cannon

Supposed Crimes LLC • Matthews, North Carolina

Published in the United States.

ISBN: 978-1-944591-57-1

www.supposedcrimes.com

This book is typeset in Goudy Old Style.

When last we visited our intrepid heroes...

LADY DOROTHY BOONE is in mourning.

In 1921, Dorothy's encounter with an ancient statue led to her body being stolen by a High Priest. DESMOND TINDALL, Dorothy's alleged fiancé, offered himself as a vessel for his mind so she could assist with her own rescue. During the course of their adventure, Dorothy regained her body at the cost of losing Desmond's. The situation was resolved in tragedy when their foe met his demise in an accident that left Desmond without a body to return to. MISS TRAFALGAR OF ABYSSINIA, the newest permanent resident of Dorothy's Threadneedle address, has taken the lead in their partnership in the months since, investigating rumors and commissions with the hope Dorothy may one day agree to pursue one of them.

Meanwhile, as the bond between members of the MNEMOSYNE SOCIETY grows stronger, BEATRICE SEK has found her personal quest at an end. Her attempts to find other Elementals forced her into an uneasy alliance with the terrorist VIRAGO, who led her to the third of their four "sisters." The three Elementals were almost immediately hijacked by a mysterious Stranger who killed them just to prove he could restore them to life, then showed Virago a vision of the future that awaited the world if all four Elementals were to unite.

Virago, shaken to her core by the visions, decided to take it upon herself to kill the other Elementals to prevent it from happening. Beatrice was forced to kill Virago in self-defense, but guilt weighs heavily on her to the point where she hardly seems like the same person she was before. When we rejoin their narrative, Trafalgar is beginning to question whether Dorothy Boone's storied career has come to a premature end.

PROLOGUE

1922

AFTER MUCH internal debate and pointless brooding, Dorothy Boone went home.

She spent weeks after Desmond's memorial haunting the hallways of her townhouse. Trafalgar and other members of the Mnemosyne Society attempted to draw her out, enticing her with stories of commissions and mysteries in need of solving, but she could not find the strength to be intrigued. Her curiosity was gone. No, more to the point, her curiosity was not strong enough to compete against her guilt, shame, and horror at what happened to her friend. Desmond was a kind man. He was innocent and had no place in her dangerous world. It was only due to his acquaintance with her that he was killed. She was the cause of so much pain in his life. How could she possibly engage in such reckless behavior knowing the consequences to those she loved?

She packed in the middle of the night, when neither Trafalgar nor Beatrice could talk her out of what needed to be done. She took a bag down from the very top shelf of the closet and carried it downstairs. She left the house just before dawn and walked to the far end of Threadneedle Street, down to Bishopsgate, where she summoned a cab. It was the driver's first fare of the day so she apologized for the long journey, but he said he would be happy to get away from the morning rush. She stared out the window at London waking up, but she saw none of it. She could only see her own reflection. Wan, ashen, with dark frames under her eyes.

The Boone estate was barely unchanged from the last time she saw it. Every blade of grass was perfectly trimmed. Every window shone with the light of the dawn. Dorothy felt a surge of nostalgia in her chest as the cab rumbled up the front drive. She grinned at the sight of the tumbling old fence where she and her cat marched off to war ("Fierce creatures, mum," she'd told her mother upon arriving home caked in mud. "I've dispatched 'um."). The low branches of the tree she fell out of, her first broken bone of many.

"Is this the place?" the driver asked, pulling to a stop in front of the porch.

"This is it," Dorothy confirmed. She paid him his fare, along with a healthy tip, and thanked him for the ride. She retrieved her bag and climbed the steps, waiting until the cab was gone before knocking.

The door opened to reveal a young man Dorothy didn't recognize, but his suit marked him unmistakably as household staff. His face was expressionless, his professionalism cracking only to show his disdain for the sort of person who would ring at such an impolite hour.

"May I help you, ma'am?"

"Ma'am?" Dorothy said. "I beg your pardon."

He stared at her without correcting himself. Dorothy squared her shoulders.

"Very well. My name is Dorothy Boone."

"That's impossible." The woman's voice echoed off the front hall. "Dorothy is my daughter's name, and she has made it quite clear that she will never again grace our abominable halls with her presence. So this couldn't possibly be Dorothy Boone."

Dorothy smiled to hide the fact the voice made her cringe. She leaned to the side and spoke around the butler. "Hello, mother. Up early, as always."

Clara Boone stepped into sight. It was barely past dawn, but she was already perfectly coiffed and dressed for the day. The years had aged her terribly, sinking her cheeks and digging pits around her eyes. The color was also faded from her hair, which was now pulled back into a severe bun. Grandmother Eula had never looked this severe or ancient even in her final days. The corners of Clara's mouth curled into a triumphant smile.

"Well." Her eyes drifted over Dorothy's outfit, taking in the dark jacket and skirt, pausing at the grey blouse as if trying to determine whether it was cut for a male or female. "I suppose it's a bit remarkable you remained stubborn for as long as you did. I've been expecting this day for years." She put a hand on the butler's shoulder. "Thank you, you may excuse us."

He dipped his head and scampered off to another area of the house. Clara took his position in the doorway, making it clear Dorothy had not yet been invited inside.

"Does this one have a name, Mother?" she asked.

"Stephen. Elmer's son. He took over after his father became ill."

Dorothy let her emotions show through. "I'm sorry to hear that. Is he all right?"

"I doubt it," Clara said, "it was years ago and he was very old. I'm certain he's passed away by now."

Dorothy started to say something but thought better of it. She pressed her lips together and put her hands behind her back.

"I see. Well..."

"I feel as if I'm making you uncomfortable. That's not my intention. I'm glad you're here. It's a relief. For so long I've felt as if I failed you, and that's been just unbearable. The thought of you in London, gallivanting off all over the globe just like your grandmother. I knew it was only a matter of time before it became too much for you, but I was beginning to fear you wouldn't survive long enough to come to your senses."

Dorothy closed her eyes. "My senses..."

"Yes. And I suppose you're surprised to learn I've been keeping tabs on you. Despite your shortcomings, you were always my daughter. Everyone else was keeping up with the news, and I had to be forewarned about what antics would be brought up at the next dinner party. Honestly, Dorothy, some of the things I have had to explain away..."

Dorothy opened her eyes. "That must have been very trying for you, Mother."

"To say the least. But the fact is that you're home now. You are not old enough to be condemned to spinsterhood, not yet. We shall reeducate you in the proper poise, dress, etiquette... we will make you the Boone daughter you were always meant to be."

"The daughter you always wanted."

Clara's smile was sincere this time. "Yes."

Dorothy stepped over the threshold and kissed Clara on the cheek. "Thank you, Mother. For the past few weeks, everyone I love has tried to talk reason with me. They've tried to remedy a pain that I couldn't even quantify. But you did exactly what I hoped you would do." She gripped her mother's shoulders. "You reminded me of who I am. More importantly, of the person I'm supposed to be."

"That's... I don't think..."

Dorothy grinned. "Goodbye, Mother. Give my love to Father when he wakes. I most likely won't be back here again for a very long time."

She turned and walked off the porch. There was no chance she could catch up with the cab, so she had a very long walk back to London ahead of her. It was fine. She could do with the exercise after being cooped up in her rooms for so long. And god, that sun! Warm and invigorating! She resisted the urge to run over to the fence and walk the post like she had so many years ago.

"Dorothy!" Her mother's voice was twisted in anger and confusion. "Get back here this instant!"

It was a good thing, to walk away from her family home. It was symbolic. The last time she left, she had someone taking her away. This time she was leaving alone. She was taking the steps of her own volition. She smiled and held her chin high.

"You didn't even take your bag!"

"Keep it!" Dorothy shouted without looking back.

It was no great loss. The silly thing was empty anyway.

Dorothy walked until she reached civilization, where she enlisted another cab to take her the rest of the way home. She still grieved for Desmond, she would probably mourn him for a very long time, but the trip home had lifted an enormous cloud from the center of her vision. She could not only see clearly again, she could see the time she had wasted in her sorrow.

She was exhausted by the time she returned to Threadneedle Street, even though the day had truly only just begun. She let herself in and, by the time she made it to the stairs, Beatrice and Trafalgar had already appeared from the kitchen. Trafalgar was dressed down in a casual tan shirt and slacks, but Beatrice was wearing her full uniform: ironed white shirt under a black vest, tan pinstriped pants, and a wide black tie. They stood shoulder to shoulder in the hallway and Dorothy fought a smile at how eager they both looked.

"Where the blazes have you been?" Beatrice demanded.

"Good morning to you as well, Trix," Dorothy said.

Trafalgar looked concerned. "We knocked on your door to see if you wanted breakfast, but you were gone."

"Certainly I haven't been acting so maudlin that you thought I'd done something rash."

Beatrice said, "We didn't know what to think. You do have enemies, you know. One of them may have discovered you were incapacitated and taken advantage."

Dorothy raised an eyebrow. "With the two of you in the house to protect me? Not very likely. But I am sorry I worried you. There was something which needed to be done, and the earlier I did it, the less chance my cowardice would overwhelm me. If I'd told either of you, you might have insisted on coming with me."

"Where did you have to go?" Trafalgar asked.

"I'll explain all in due time. For now, I'd like to freshen up. I ended up walking much more than I expected." She put a hand on Beatrice's shoulder. "Give me about ten minutes and then come meet me in my office. There's something I think we should talk about."

Beatrice nodded uncertainly.

"I apologize again for alarming you both. But this morning was a rousing success, and I think things will be getting back to normal around here very soon."

Trafalgar allowed herself a hopeful smile. "That is very welcome news. We'll save you some breakfast."

"Thank you."

Dorothy felt their eyes on her as she continued upstairs.

She undressed in her room, washed away the sweat from her walk and the grimy feeling that came from speaking to her family, and put on a fresh outfit. She put on more cosmetics than she was usually comfortable with, but until healthy eating and a solid sleep schedule could return her natural shine, she felt it was necessary. Once she felt presentable, she went into her office to find Beatrice was already waiting for her. She was perched on the couch, one leg crossed over the other with her hands folded on top of them. The sun shone through the window behind her, illuminating the subtle tint of brown in her hair.

"You could have finished your breakfast."

"I ate something earlier," Beatrice said. "Even if I hadn't, I believe I'd be far more interested in what you need to tell me."

Dorothy sighed. "Right." She crossed the room to take a position behind her desk. "I believe the time has come to terminate your employment."

Beatrice went very still. "Beg pardon?"

"It's quite past time, to be frank."

"Have I done something to... i-is this about what I did to Virago?"

"No," Dorothy said softly. "That was self-defense. This has nothing to do with your performance in the job. It's the nature of the job itself. My majordomo, my butler, my housekeeper." She grimaced and rested her hands on top of the desk. "I went home this morning to the Boone estates. The footman answered the door. He's the son of the man who worked for us when I grew up. I didn't even know he had a son. I don't even know their bloody surname! I was disgusted at the idea my family could treat a man so poorly, like he was property. And I realized I had put you in the same position."

Beatrice said, "Bushwa."

"I know our relationship goes far beyond the typical mistress-servant roles, but that is why it has to end. It's unseemly. It's wrong. To keep you in a subservient role—"

"I'm your equal," Beatrice interrupted, "and you have *never* treated me as anything less. Even when you discovered me robbing your home, you showed compassion. You gave me a home. You gave me purpose. Please don't take that from me now, Dorothy."

Dorothy said, "You answer my door, drive my car, and tend to my household."

"I live under your roof, eat your food, and share your bed. If anything, I am overcompensated."

Dorothy screwed up her lips and looked down at the table. "When I walked in and saw you wearing that uniform..."

Beatrice gripped the tie with one hand, tugging the knot loose. "Shall I take it off?"

"No! I... not that I'm opposed to the idea in principle." She smiled, and Beatrice returned it. "I don't want anyone to look at us and think you haven't earned your place at my side."

Beatrice let go of her tie and stepped closer. "I don't care how they see me. The only thing that matters is how you see me." She stepped around the desk and put her hand on top of Dorothy's. "Do you see me as just an employee? A servant?"

"Never."

"If you did fire me," she asked, trailing her fingers up Dorothy's sleeve, "would you see me banished from your life?"

"Of course not," Dorothy said. "That was never the plan, Trix. I was merely..."

Beatrice shushed her, pressed two fingers against her lips. "So if I'm going to be in your life regardless, then I might as well keep up with my chores. I quite enjoy most of them, if I'm being honest. They're relaxing. And as for everything else... protecting your home, protecting you... I would be doing that no matter what."

Dorothy pressed her lips to Beatrice's fingers. "And the... other things?"

"Were you paying me for those activities?"

Dorothy laughed huskily. "Oh, Trix, I have deep pockets, but even I couldn't have afforded what even a single night with you is worth."

Beatrice stepped closer, grinning. "I should be paying you."

"Shall I raise your hourly rate?"

"We should probably just call it even, I think."

Beatrice finally closed the distance and kissed her. Dorothy hadn't bothered to put her hair back up after washing up so it was free and available for Beatrice to grip it, twisting her wrist until it was wrapped around her hand. Dorothy opened her mouth and accepted Beatrice's flickering tongue, turning so her hips were pressing Beatrice against the edge of the desk. They had made love a few times since Desmond's death, since Beatrice used her power to kill Virago, but this morning felt different. It felt like before.

"There~" The next word was swallowed by another kiss, and Dorothy smiled. "There is a certain subservient position that you've never objected to. But in light of our conversation, perhaps you would allow me to do the honors." Her hand moved to the fasteners of Beatrice's trousers.

Beatrice smiled and braced her hands on the desk. "As you wish, ma'am."

Dorothy grinned and got onto her knees as she pulled the uniform pants down.

***

Trafalgar hesitated on the landing. She was concerned, even though Dorothy had seemed relaxed and calm when she arrived. She actually looked immensely better than she had in the past few weeks. A winter had set in Dorothy's eyes and colored her mood. There were no jokes, no laughter or music lifting from the den during the long nights she'd been spending hidden away there with her books.

She wished she knew what Dorothy and Trix were discussing behind closed doors. They tended to be very open around her, perhaps too open in some cases. She blushed when she remembered some of the conversations they'd had over breakfast. They loved to recount the origin of bruises and "love-bites" they inflicted on one another. Lately, however, it had been a struggle to get more than three words out of Dorothy, and Beatrice became taciturn in response. It was a highly awkward situation and one she felt had been on the verge of collapse for days.

Trafalgar moved closer to the door and listened. Was that a sob? She worried her bottom lip with her teeth, one hand flat against the wall and the other resting on the knob. Perhaps Dorothy felt closer to Beatrice. It made sense, of course, as they'd known one another longer. But she wanted Dorothy to know she had more than one confidant in the house. A second sob came from within the office, and Trafalgar was convinced of what had to be done. Dorothy needed her support.

She twisted the knob and stepped into the office.

Beatrice was sitting on the desk with her back to the door. One bare leg was up, knee bent. One of Dorothy's hands had vanished under the tails of Beatrice's shirt, while the other... well, Trafalgar could guess where the other was, even if the idea made her blush. The sobs she'd heard from outside were louder now and it was obvious what they really were.

For a moment, Trafalgar remained where she was. Her interest wasn't purely prurient. Seeing her engaged in this activity was an enormously welcome sign that things might be returning to normal. She was still considering this when the top of Dorothy lifted her head and looked past the curve of Beatrice's hip. One eyebrow was lifted.

"You're more than welcome to watch, Miss Trafalgar," Dorothy said, "but you might want to find somewhere more comfortable as I intend to be here for a while."

Trafalgar cleared her throat. "I'll leave you to it."

Beatrice twisted at the waist and smiled. "Bye, Trafalgar."

"Good-bye, Trix. Ah... e-enjoy yourselves, ladies..."

She closed the door and retreated down the stairs, laughing in spite of her embarrassment. Yes, it was inappropriate of them to engage in such behavior even in a semi-private space like Dorothy's office. And yes, it was inconsiderate of Dorothy to run off to god-knew-where without explaining herself to put their minds at ease.

And yes, she was furious at herself for being embarrassed by Dorothy's teasing. In other words, it was just like the old days, and it was a very encouraging sign that normalcy was on the horizon.

Chapter One

Dorothy's arrangement with the Yeovil Street Gentlemen's Club was simple: the first man to defeat her in fencing would have the honor of not only escorting her from the premises, but he would be responsible for proving women don't belong in their esteemed company. On her first visit, when she was still a ward of her grandmother, she asked to face their weakest swordsman. "After all, if I cannot beat him then surely I pose no threat to any of you." Her challenge played to their egos, and every man present knew it was a mere formality. There was no chance she could defeat one of them. The point was moot. So surely one bout with a girl was a small price to pay for silence from any other woman asking to join their ranks.

There was some dissent about who, exactly, was their weakest man. Eventually one was chosen, and he angrily stepped forward prepared to prove his mettle. He glared at her through their salute, eyes locked on her until he pulled his mask down to obscure his face. Dorothy was wearing a borrowed uniform, awkward and bulky and too large.

Her first match was over in seconds and an utter embarrassment. She was too cocky and prepared her attack within striking distance, suffering a blow to her sword arm which left her shaken. Her opponent, seeing an opportunity to save face and defend his club's discriminatory policy all at the same time, showed her no mercy. She left the *piste* to the sound of cheers and offers to buy the victor drinks. They had stopped thinking about her by the time she was out of the room, so none of them noticed that she took the borrowed foil with her.

Dorothy practiced at home with her grandmother. She read books and watched public performances to see how it looked in practice. She learned it like a foreigner picking up a new language. She immersed herself in the conversation of those who spoke it fluently: lunge, parry, counter-parry, riposte, retreat. She left marks on her grandmother's coatrack which remained to this day, evidence of poor attacks and failed feints.

When she returned to Yeovil Street two months later, she made the same offer. She would do her best against their worst, and the first man to defeat her could kick her out of the club. The same man who had originally defeated her stepped forward again. Dorothy raised her weapon to salute him. He smiled, already victorious in his mind. She winked and lowered her mask, dropped her sword, and the match began.

She made short work of him. His overconfidence led to several sloppy mistakes which she was now adept enough to take advantage of.

One of the men grumbled, "I believe the time has come for you to take your leave, young lady."

"I will leave when my conditions have been met." She held out her blade and swept the point slowly across the crowd of spectators. "Which of you will earn the right to dismiss me from this place, hmm? I'll stand against any man willing to face me."

An older man with ash blonde whiskers stepped forward. There was no chance he was a novice, but she nonetheless accepted his challenge. He was brutal and mean in his attacks, which gave her more openings than she'd expected. His rage made him sloppy and he forgot his training. He swung his foil like he was trying to swat a fly. Dorothy took advantage of his mistakes but she was still no match for him. Eventually his skills won out and she had to admit defeat. He removed his mask and tossed it aside, not looking at her when he said, "Now get the hell out of here, and don't come back."

"Frightened of a rematch?" Dorothy said. "Worried now that I know your tricks, I'll be able to win the next time we face each other?"

"Know your place, girl."

"I know my place," Dorothy said. "I just have to get past its gatekeepers." She tucked her mask under her sword arm, extending the opposite hand to the man who had defeated her. "I believe it's customary to shake hands after a match."

He finally looked at her. After a long pause, he walked back, gripped her hand, and squeezed. Dorothy refused to flinch or even blink as she met his gaze.

"This is not a sport for women," he said under his breath.

"Not yet," Dorothy said, "but I believe all things can be improved with enough effort."

He dropped her hand.

"Thank you for the matches, gentlemen. I look forward to our next bout."

The next time she visited, she was defeated by her first opponent. A month after that, she survived three in a row before she lost. She quickly learned that every man she faced, no matter their skill, shared the same fault: they treated their matches like a battle. Dorothy knew it was more graceful than that. It was dancing, only with a winner. Eventually she was winning matches against anyone who took up her challenge. She left when she was tired, and not a moment before.

Now she had been coming so long that she was senior to some of the official members. It became a rite of passage. Every man wanted to be the one who sent her packing once and for all. Unfortunately by this point, Dorothy was more skilled than any of them could hope to be. They were crude, amateurish. Some of them managed to win due to superior strength, sheer dumb luck, or a bad day on Dorothy's part. When it came to skill, however, the men of the Yeovil Street Gentlemen's Club simply no longer provided a challenge for her.

It had been quite some time since she took up a blade, but she returned in an attempt to get back to normalcy. Going out was a chance to get some fresh air as well as some exercise. She was a bit rusty but her muscle memory served her well. She finished a series of four bouts, the last of them against a young man who likely didn't yet need a razor, and went into the locker room to change back into her street clothes. The fresh-faced boy had used some decidedly adult language when she defeated him and refused to shake her hand. Disappointing, but it reflected worse on him than her. It was also disappointing that she might have to find a new club. If she couldn't find worthy opponents, she might have to give up the sport altogether.

Dorothy took a seat on the bench in the center of the changing area. She unfastened her jacket collar and then began working the row of buttons that ran down the left side of her chest.

"Quite ironic," she muttered. "Men will have finally succeeded in banishing me from the sport simply through inadequacy."

"Perhaps you should begin your own club," a woman said from the far side of the room. Her voice echoed off the gleaming lockers and tile floor. "Train other women. Allow your students to surpass their master."

"An interesting idea," Dorothy said. "One worth pursuing should I survive long enough to see retirement." She stood up and removed her jacket, reaching up to unfasten her breastplate. "If you're the delicate sort, I should warn you that nudity is imminent and you might wish to remain where you are."

The woman appeared at the end of the row of lockers. She was Indian, though her accent was more American than British. She wore a sleeveless silk blouse, its low-cut V made more modest by a thrice-layered string of pearls. Her black eyes were furthered darkened by subtle smudges of mascara. She was wearing a bowler but removed it as soon as she stepped into sight, revealing purple-black hair pinned back in a way that almost made it look like a masculine cut. The woman leaned against the white tile of the wall and crossed her arms over her chest. She offered a cheeky smile as proof she had taken Dorothy's warning as an invitation, nodding at the locker.

"You aren't worried about the men stealing your clothes while you're fighting?"

"They've tried it a few times." Dorothy returned the woman's smile and removed her shirt. "But I was undeterred, and they decided it wasn't worth the trouble. It turns out that young men regularly disposing of women's clothing eventually face a lot of uncomfortable questions."

"I'll bet."

Dorothy was down to her underthings now, which prompted her to change the subject. "When I've reached this state of undress with a woman, I generally at least know her name."

The woman raised an eyebrow. "Aha. So the rumors are true."

"There are rumors about me?" Dorothy feigned shock.

"In certain circles. Don't worry, you're spoken of very highly." The tip of her tongue darted against the corner of her mouth.

Interesting, Dorothy thought. "You still haven't told me who you are."

"My name is Riya Lennox. And of course there's no need for you to introduce yourself. The infamous Lady Boone, seeker of myths and slayer of beasts."

"I've never slain a beast," Dorothy said, "unless you count certain men with beastly behavior. I did once do battle with the Minotaur, but we were able to reason with one another and let each other walk away intact."

Lennox grinned and moved to sit on the bench behind Dorothy. "You know how it is with legends. Truth wrapped up in fiction."

"Legend?" Dorothy continued disrobing. She decided if Lennox wasn't going to make an issue of it, neither would she. "I don't know if I quite qualify for that."

"Give it time," Lennox said. "I apologize for approaching you like this, but I wanted to speak with you directly. I suppose I could have gone to the Society or spoken to Miss Trafalgar, but I had the feeling the final say would come from you. So why not save us all some time?"

"You have me intrigued, Miss Lennox. What can I do for you?"

Lennox said, "It's what I can do for you, Lady Boone. You simply have to keep doing what you're doing."

"Undressing?"

"Well yes, that. And thank you, by the way, it's quite an enjoyable show."

Dorothy smirked with her back turned so Lennox couldn't see it.

"But I was referring to your adventuring. Joining up with the others in the Mnemosyne Society has granted you some freedom, but you're all spending money faster than you can replace it. Within a few years, long-term excursions across the globe will be all but impossible. You'll be scrounging for coins to pay cab fare to the British Museum."

"There have been discussions among the Society about how to boost commissions. The Keepings have spoken with several potential patrons who are interested in supporting our explorations."

Lennox said, "Indeed they have. And I'm here to end their quest." She stood and moved so Dorothy could see her. "I wish to finance you."

"That's very generous of you, but the idea of a single person funding--"

"Twenty-five thousand pounds," Lennox said. "Annually. Granted to the Mnemosyne Society to use as they see fit."

Dorothy couldn't think. Couldn't speak. She suddenly wished she wasn't in her underthings. She searched Lennox face for signs of mockery or deception but saw only hopeful excitement.

"Now you see why I didn't want to make this offer to just anyone. I know you trust your fellow Society members, and you share a home with Miss Trafalgar, but this amount of money could make anyone greedy. You used your grandmother's fortune to fund your work. You were the one who pushed to create the Society in the first place. You put the work ahead of your own glory. That is why I knew I could trust you."

Dorothy said, "And what would you want in return?"

Lennox shrugged. "Nothing outside of your comfort zone."

"A kiss?"

Lennox's smile widened and her voice dropped to a more seductive purr. "Ah, no, Lady Boone. Should your lips ever grace mine, I pray that it will be of your own free will."

Dorothy raised an eyebrow. She put her blouse on and began working the buttons. "So there is a caveat to taking your offer."

"Not only that, I can't tell you what it is. Not yet. One day I will ask you to undertake a mission for me. It will be harrowing, and the sort of thing I couldn't possibly ask for unless I was calling in an enormous favor. Hence the money. I can only swear that what I ask of you will not be outside your realm of comfort."

"Not exactly reassuring," Dorothy said.

"Unfortunately, it's all I can offer." She replaced the hat upon her head and took Dorothy's hand, bowing to kiss the knuckles. "Take some time to consider it. Talk to your compatriots. I would invite you to investigate me, but you'll find nothing. You only have my word that I am a friend, and a follower of your excellent work."

Dorothy said, "It is a great deal of money."

Lennox smiled, her expression unreadable. "I've never believed that a person's passion should be hindered by something as ridiculous as a lack of funds. You and the Society are unlocking the mysteries of this world. In doing so, you may very well save the future." She touched her finger to the brim of her hat and dipped her chin. "I look forward to your answer, Lady

Boone." She stepped around the row of lockers, once again out of sight.

"How will I find you?" Dorothy called after her.

"I'll find you," Lennox promised, her voice echoing as it had when she first arrived.

Dorothy stood in the once-again empty locker room, replaying the conversation in her mind and tripping up when she reached the number. Twenty-five thousand pounds. Annually. The things the Society could do with coffers like that...

She blew air out through her lips and continued dressing. She would definitely have to call an emergency meeting of the Society that evening.

CHAPTER TWO

CECIL DUBOURNE was the first to respond after Dorothy finished recounting her conversation with Riya Lennox. He had been sitting backwards on a stool, elbows resting on the bar, but he leaned forward and clapped his hands together. "I say we take her up on it, buy everyone houses, and call it a year."

The rest of the Mnemosyne Society was gathered in the main room of the Inkwell. The Keepings, Agnes and Leonard, were seated together on one side of a booth, with Cora Hyde across from them. Abraham Strode went behind the bar, initially to pour himself a drink and then to savor it while he listened to Dorothy's tale. Trafalgar was also sitting at the bar, but she'd taken a stool as far from Cecil as possible without being obviously rude. Beatrice, the newest full member of the Society, was sitting on the stairs leading up to the second floor of the tavern.

"The money would be for the Society," Dorothy said. "It would go toward funding expeditions, hiring crews, shipping costs, the rent on this place."

"We could all buy houses and have enough left over for the boring stuff," Abraham said. "It's an almost ludicrous amount of money, especially from an utter stranger."

"It's ludicrous once," Leonard Keeping said. "But this 'Miss Lennox' made the offer to pay the same amount annually. There are entire countries which couldn't make such an extravagant promise."

Agnes nodded in agreement with her husband. "I think it's clear we're dealing with a confidence woman. Not a very good one, at that. The key to a good lie is believability. She can't possibly expect us to take her at her word."

Dorothy raised an eyebrow and looked at the floor.

Trafalgar said, "You believe her?"

"I do. I'm not entirely sure why. You're absolutely correct, Mrs. Keeping. A con would know to keep their lie believable. And there was something about the confidence with which she made the offer. It was as if the amount was nothing to her. Less than nothing. I truly believe that if we agree to work with her, the money will be made available."

A line appeared between Agnes' eyebrows, but she didn't argue.

"And there are no other conditions on the money?"

The voice seemed to come from nowhere, and everyone in the room looked somewhere different. Dorothy looked at Beatrice, who was looking at a spot near the window. Ivy Sever, cursed with invisibility, had arrived at the meeting nude and unable to be tracked. But Dorothy trusted Beatrice's senses and so directed her response to that spot.

"Only that I make myself available to her at some future date. I would of course take the debt upon myself, since I'm the one who received the offer to begin with."

Abraham said, "Well, if we all benefit from the money, then we should share the risk equally."

Leonard nodded. "Agreed."

Cecil ran a hand through his hair. "Well, maybe we can wait until we know what the favor is before we jump in with both feet, eh?"

"That's more than fair," Dorothy said.

"How long do we have to decide?" Cora asked.

Agnes said, "And does our answer need to be unanimous?"

"A majority should be fine," Leonard said. "Dorothy is willing to take on the risk. So even if a nay vote is outnumbered, the only consequence is they benefit from the money."

Cora said, "So we won't require a consensus, but those who vote 'aye' will share the burden of answering this Lennox woman's call. There's no reason Dorothy must shoulder it herself."

Dorothy nodded her thanks to Cora, who dipped her head in acknowledgement.

"We don't need to vote immediately. I've no idea when Miss Lennox will reappear, but I'm certain we can at least sleep on it."

There was a knock on the door. Everyone turned to look at it, then refocused on Dorothy.

"Then again, perhaps she's the impatient sort."

Leonard was closest, so he stood and answered the knock. Standing on the other side was no Riya Lennox, but a man Dorothy hadn't seen before. A quick survey of the room indicated that everyone else was just as confused about who he was.

"My apologies," Leonard said, "but this isn't actually a working pub."

"Oh, I'm aware. I'm not looking for a drink. I was told I would find the

Nemo-scene Society here."

"Ne-mah-se-ne," Dorothy corrected. "May I ask how you came across that information?"

He fumbled in his coat pocket and produced a newspaper clipping. It had been folded so many times that the creases looked soft and ready to break apart. "I read about the drowned necropolis you discovered, and I've been following the progress of other expeditions looking to continue the research you started. I thought perhaps I could engage your services. May I come in?"

Leonard looked at Dorothy, who nodded her approval. She looked toward the empty space where she believed Ivy had last been standing.

"Keep an eye on him, Ms. Sever," Dorothy said under her breath.

"Already doing it," Ivy said, much closer than Dorothy expected her to be.

The stranger came inside and offered his hand to Leonard. "Bertram Rees," he said. "It's a pleasure to make your acquaintance."

Leonard shook his hand. "Leonard Keeping. My wife, Agnes." He completed the introductions, gesturing to each person in turn. He hesitated before naming Ivy, and Dorothy gave a quick negative shake of her head. "And lastly, the woman responsible for bringing us all together: the Lady Dorothy Boone."

"Hello, Mr. Rees," Dorothy said.

"Charmed." He turned slightly, presenting his face to Leonard and Cecil while Dorothy was looking at his shoulder. "Thank you for agreeing to see me. I wasn't certain of the etiquette in this sort of matter. I couldn't find any information about whether you took appointments, or how one would set one up if you did."

"It's quite all right," Dorothy said. "You're fortunate to find us all gathered tonight."

"Mm," he said, glancing in her direction before focusing on the men again.

Dorothy stifled a sigh. This was to be expected, but that didn't mean she had to like it. Leonard looked at Dorothy as if he wanted to press the issue, but she gave a quick shake of her head. No sense in making a scene unless it became necessary.

"I represent the Royal Geographical Society. Two years ago, we commissioned a cartographer named Captain Felix Neville to find a mythical river called the Pratear. The expedition maintained their correspondence until about a year ago, when we stopped receiving updates from them. We believed they may have simply moved into an area where they weren't able to send messages, but the more time passed, the more concerned we became. After six months, we began debating our options."

Dorothy picked up Abraham's beer glass. He watched her but said nothing as she carried it to Rees. He was still addressing the men in the room. She placed the glass near his right hand.

"Oh, thank you," he muttered.

"My pleasure." She stepped around him and returned to her spot by the bar.

He resumed his speech. "Several of us believed it would be best to cut our losses. Simply move on to the next commission. But the majority of us have faith that Neville and his men are still alive and merely lost or too deep into their expedition to bother with correspondence. If we were to move on, we may be leaving them stranded when they finally do reappear. We asked around and it would seem the men in this room comprise the best explorers London has to offer. A vote was taken and the group decided that you would be our last resort. We will fund an expedition for you to follow in Neville's footsteps to see if you can uncover his fate."

"We'll do it."

Rees looked at Dorothy in a way that proved she stopped existing in his mind when she wasn't speaking. He smiled and looked almost bashful.

"With all due respect - Lady Boone, wasn't it? - I suspect the gentlemen would like a bit more information before making their decision."

"I have all the information I need." Dorothy held up the small book she'd been perusing while he spoke. "Your man, Neville, departed from London two years ago aboard the *HMS Herald.* They arrived at Belém, Brazil, where a local guide escorted them into the rainforest." She put the journal down again and thumbed through the pages. "I appreciate the summarization of Neville's letters back home, but I would like to have the originals so I can examine them while traveling to South America."

Rees stared at the book, then pressed a hand against the pocket of his suit jacket. "How did~?"

"When she gave you the drink," Trafalgar said, smirking proudly.

"You stole from me?"

Dorothy looked at him, the picture of innocence. "Well, I can't take all the blame, Mr. Rees. You're the one who rendered me invisible. I simply took advantage."

Rees looked around the room as if he expected someone to reprimand her. Instead he saw only unmasked amusement. Cora touched a knuckle to the corner of her eye, and Beatrice was smiling at Dorothy with what she could only categorize as arousal. He clearly deduced who was truly in charge from their reactions and turned so he was facing her fully.

"I see. Lady Boone."

"Yes?"

"I apologize for my assumption. I meant no disrespect."

Dorothy said, "Apology accepted." She closed the journal. "And I apologize for taking the journal without permission, but it seemed the best way to expedite the process. As I said, we accept your proposition on the basis we come to acceptable terms. Compensation, for instance."

"Of course," Rees said.

"You may discuss those matters with Miss Trafalgar and the Keepings. If we come to an accord, we'll begin planning our expedition as soon as possible. As for the original letters from Neville and his team...?"

"I'll have them forwarded to... to *your* address, Lady Boone."

She smiled sweetly. "Beatrice, please make sure Mr. Rees has the proper address."

"Yes, ma'am," Beatrice said.

Beatrice's tone made certain parts of Dorothy flush and quake. She composed herself before speaking again.

"In the meantime, I'll keep the journal to begin forming our plan of action."

"Ah, very... very well. The RGS thanks you for your assistance in this matter. We'll be in touch."

He made his farewells, arranged a time and place where he could talk logistics with Trafalgar and Leonard, and made a hasty escape back into the evening. Leonard closed the door behind him and smiled at Dorothy.

"You are a caution."

"I prefer to think of myself as a walking education for those who might require one." She caught Trafalgar's eye and tapped the cover of the journal. "You should take a look at this as well. I assume you'll be accompanying me on the trip."

Trafalgar said, "It would be my honor. Who else will be coming with us?"

Abraham held his hands up, palm-out. "Equatorial rainforest? Not for me. But have fun with the bugs and snakes, ladies."

Ivy's voice came from near the door. "I think it goes without saying that I'm staying here. I'm a local girl. Wouldn't know what to do in the world."

"I'm afraid at our age," Agnes Keeping said, "we would be more of a hindrance than a benefit. Quite a shame. I've never been to Brazil."

"Of course you have," Leonard said. "Six days on the Amazon River. Although you can be forgiven for not remembering where we were."

She smiled sweetly at him. "That wasn't me, dear."

He looked at her and then his face blanched. "Oh. Of course."

Agnes laughed and poked the tip of her husband's nose.

Cora Hyde said, "I believe the time has come for me to return to the field. My skills as a linguist could prove invaluable with the local tribes. If you're willing to have me, of course."

"Always," Dorothy said. Cora had remained in country for the past few years after a tragic expedition which ended in the unexplained death of her entire team. She'd spent that time brushing up on her mythology, history, and language skills. When she finally checked herself out of the mental hospital, she had seemed robust and revitalized, even if her dark hair had a few more streaks of premature silver than before. If she believed herself ready for another outing, Dorothy would consider herself lucky to have her.

Cecil said, "Sounds like this is turning into a trip for ladies only. Not that it would be dull, but I suppose I should bow out as well."

Abraham snorted. "As if you could handle the rainforest any better than me. Don't blame gender, you're staying because you hate to be uncomfortable."

Cecil raised his glass. "Don't hate me for what I am."

Leonard looked at Dorothy. "So once again, it seems the heavy lifting of the Mnemosyne Society will be undertaken by Trafalgar and Boone."

"We're sticking with her name first...?" Dorothy asked.

"You object?" Trafalgar said.

"No, no. Just making sure. It has a certain ring to it."

Trafalgar grinned. "I have to agree. Besides, it isn't as if we're printing up business cards."

"Right." Dorothy gently lobbed the journal to Trafalgar, who caught it easily. "We'll get to work reading up on Mr. Felix Neville. And all of us will take the time to consider Riya Lennox's generous offer to fund our work. And I believe that will be the end of a very productive meeting. Any objections?"

No one did. Dorothy rapped her knuckles on the bar top.

"Meeting adjourned."

CHAPTER THREE

RIYA LENNOX was true to her word on at least one count: there was no evidence the woman even existed. Cecil and the Keepings had used their contacts to see what they could discover about her. During the two weeks Dorothy and Trafalgar arranged their trip to Brazil, they waited for word. They asked their usual network of ears and whispers to see what they could find out about the mystery woman. Finally the spies came back with a definitive report of... nothing. No woman matching her description, using the name Lennox or otherwise, was recorded in London at any time in the past five years. Agnes Keeping revealed her lack of success in Dorothy's parlor the day before they were scheduled to set sail. Dorothy took the opportunity to take a break from packing and have tea with her friend in the parlor.

Agnes revealed, her frustration evident, that she had gone so far as to inquire about immigration records for Indian families. There were many, of course, and a great number of them with daughters, but none were the right age.

"Perhaps I was off," Dorothy suggested. She was leaning against the edge of her desk, feet crossed at the ankles and arms folded casually over her stomach. "I could have guessed her age wrong. Perhaps five years, even ten..."

"Unless the woman you saw was a mature ten or a very well-preserved ninety-one, I doubt it." Agnes shrugged. She was sitting on the divan near the window, half-turned so she could see the doorway in her periphery. "A woman with the means she purports to have shouldn't be this difficult to find."

Dorothy said, "Or perhaps she uses those means to ensure she remains in the shadows."

Agnes considered that, then nodded. "We'll keep up our efforts while you ladies are on your mission. But I warn you to anticipate disappointment."

"I consider myself warned." Dorothy liked the time she spent with Agnes. The older woman reminded her of her grandmother; brave, blunt, and unwilling to take crap from anyone. She refused to let anyone judge her by her age. Anyone who underestimated her was quickly taught the error of their ways. "Have you and Leonard given any more thought to her offer? You need the money less than any of us."

Agnes said, "We're well off, true. But we do prefer to spend someone else's money whenever possible. That's the quickest way to stay rich." She smiled and offered a wink. "I worry about what the eventual cost may be. One can claim charity all day long, but there will always be some string attached. This Lennox woman admitted as much."

Dorothy pursed her lips and nodded. "Yes, and quite a large one. I wish we had a way of contacting her, or at least knew how long we had to discuss our options."

Agnes finished her tea and stood, placing the cup and saucer on the corner of Dorothy's desk. "The solution is simple. If this Riya Lennox returns before we've come to a final decision, tell her no. Nothing good has ever come from rushing a decision this large."

"You are quite right. Thank you, Agnes."

"Safe travels, Dorothy. We shall await word of your adventures, as always."

Dorothy saw her off and returned to her room to finish packing. The suitcase was where she'd left it on the foot of the bed, but it had been filled in her absence. Beatrice was in the process of closing it when Dorothy caught her.

"I thought we spoke about you doing menial tasks around the house," Dorothy scolded gently.

"We did," Beatrice said. "We agreed I would only do the things which I chose to do. I wanted to do this because I know your time is short. You and Trafalgar leave tomorrow morning."

Dorothy embraced Beatrice from behind and kissed her neck. "Indeed we do."

"I think there are better ways to spend the time you have remaining in London." She took Dorothy's hands from where they rested on her stomach and guided them lower.

"You could always come with us."

Dorothy made quick work of Beatrice's belt, then unfastened her trousers. Beatrice straightened her posture as Dorothy's deft right hand disappeared into the folds of the clothes. She reached back and rested her hands on Dorothy's hips.

"My place is here." Beatrice's voice was softer with her arousal. "Protecting your home."

"I want you at my side."

"You want me beneath you."

Dorothy smiled. "Yes, occasionally. But in a general sense, you are my right hand."

"Lucky hand," Beatrice said.

"Yes." Dorothy nipped Beatrice's earlobe. "You've determined your powers are earth-based. What better place to explore that potential than a rainforest?"

"What more terrifying place," Beatrice corrected. She reached down, covering Dorothy's hand with her own, guiding her movements. "I can feel the power tugging at me even when I'm in the middle of a city. If I venture into the country, it becomes like a church bell ringing just on the other side of a hill. I shudder to think what might happen if I venture into a completely undeveloped world."

Dorothy kissed Beatrice's hair and moved down to her neck. Her free hand was now at Beatrice's chest. "I would be there for you," she promised. "I would catch you if you fell."

"You would be there as a potential, inadvertent target."

"I'm willing to risk it."

"I'm not." Beatrice was breathing heavily now. "I will remain here, keeping the home fires burning until you return."

Dorothy said, "If that is truly what you wish, I will abide by your decision. But I shall miss you terribly."

"And I, you. Please, Dorothy..."

Dorothy rested her cheek against the smooth shoulder of Beatrice's shirt and finished what she was doing, eyes closed so she could enjoy ever tremble and quiet gasp Beatrice made. Afterward, when Dorothy freed her hand, Beatrice turned to face her. She kissed Dorothy's lips and touched her hair.

"Don't be gone too long, my love."

Dorothy turned her head to kiss Beatrice's palm. "You'll be in my heart every day. Every evening."

"I'd better be. And if you happen to find someone to share your bed, you know that I won't object. But just to be certain your heart remains with me..." Beatrice nodded toward the suitcase. "I packed a few items to keep my memory fresh, no matter what wild local women may have to offer."

"I can't wait to discover those treasures." She kissed the corners of Beatrice's mouth. "Now, since I planned to be packing all afternoon, it would seem I have at least one free hour. Perhaps you can refresh my memory of you in a more concrete manner."

Beatrice's fingers moved to the collar of Dorothy's blouse. "Let's see what we can come up with."

Dorothy put her hand in the small of Beatrice's back and allowed herself to be pulled onto the bed, knocking the suitcase out of the way in the process.

Trafalgar glanced up at the sound of a thud against the floor, but she didn't let it distract her. Agnes Keeping had left, Dorothy and Beatrice were in the same area of the house, and there was a loud noise. It didn't require much deduction to conclude what was happening. Her housemates had a... healthy physical appreciation for each other. She was in the study, which was inconveniently located beneath the master bedroom, but she was confident focusing on work would help her ignore any sounds coming from above.

She hadn't quite expected the level of their promiscuity when she accepted Dorothy's invitation to move in. Sex had never been one of her driving interests. She had gone to bed with two men in the past, not counting her dalliance at sea - she still blushed when that memory surfaced - but those encounters had been what she considered physical outbursts, momentary lapses of lust which were sated and forgotten.

But Dorothy and Beatrice... there was something more there. It may have started as lust, but now it was something much more. She admitted her own prejudices originally led her to believe their relationship was only carnal. They were both women, surely there was nothing romantic about what they were doing. She'd since changed her opinion. The love and devotion they shared was stronger than some married couples she'd known. If the relationship ever became public, Trafalgar knew she would stand to defend them.

For now, though, she would respect their relationship by ignoring the sounds coming from upstairs and focusing on her research. While Dorothy had been searching for Riya Lennox, Trafalgar had spent her time looking into Felix Neville, the lost captain of the *HMS Herald*. A military man and the son of a military man, Neville seemed to have used his service as a means to travel the world. The RGS had sent over a wealth of letters and journals from his time stationed in Africa and the Philippines which painted the picture of a man more concerned with learning about local cultures than war. He eventually left the service and began exploring as a private citizen. He was a widower with three sons, the eldest of which had accompanied him on the latest ill-fated expedition.

Dorothy had a plethora of maps, and Trafalgar easily found one which covered the area Neville planned to explore. It didn't seem very removed from civilization, but she knew the forest could be deceiving. Ten feet in the wrong direction could prove fatal even to the most experienced explorer.

Trafalgar mapped the route the *Herald*'s crew had taken into the jungle according to Mr. Rees' data. She would leave the details to Dorothy and whoever captained their ship, but she assumed their rescue mission would likely follow the same landmarks. She was uncertain whether they would make the first leg of their journey by air or by sea. An airship could get them to Brazil in three days, whereas an ocean liner might take closer to a week. Whatever they lost in time would be regained in comfort. But she was certain Neville and his team would appreciate their haste. She made a note to Dorothy that they should elect to travel by air.

She was nervous. She liked to present herself as a world traveler, but the truth was she'd rarely been to the west. She took jobs in Africa, the Middle East, China. Her few experiences in the Americas were brief and unmemorable. She had always been so focused on the mission that she'd never gotten a chance to appreciate the fact she was crossing an ocean. This time it would be difficult to ignore that vast and endless stretch of water.

She was no fan of the water since her experience in the necropolis. She remembered being in that cavern, very aware of how thin their lifeline back to the surface was. She'd handled the experience well in the moment but now it was encroaching on her nightmares. Some nights she was back there, alone in a freezing stone grave, Dorothy's dead body slumped against the wall next to her, and she was overcome with a feeling of certain doom.

A door opened on the upper floor and she heard Dorothy's laughter, followed by footsteps on the stairs. She looked up from her work as Dorothy breezed past the doorway to the study only to backtrack and lean against the wall. She was wearing Beatrice's uniform shirt, buttoned wrong, and apparently nothing else. The shirt was long enough to almost serve as a dress, but Trafalgar was surprised by Dorothy's bare legs and feet. Her hair was also loose and tangled around her face.

"There you are," Dorothy said. "Trix and I were discussing dinner plans. She doesn't feel like cooking so I thought we would make an evening of it. I wanted to know if we should make the reservation for two or three."

"While I appreciate the offer, I wouldn't want my presence to limit your options."

"Why~" The humor vanished from Dorothy's face. "Any establishment that won't serve you will also never serve me. If that's your only consideration..."

Trafalgar smiled. "I would be happy to join you."

"We're not planning to eat for at least another hour, so you'll have plenty of time to finish what you're working on." Dorothy came into the room, head tilted as she examined the books and notes spread out on the table. "What *are* you working on?"

"Research for our upcoming expedition. Planning a route, learning what I can about Captain Neville from what the RGS provided."

"Fascinating." Dorothy leaned down to examine the books. Trafalgar found herself oddly transfixed by Dorothy's legs and general state of undress. "Will you be bringing this along with you on the trip?"

"Might as well," Trafalgar said. "We'll have to find some way to fill the travel time. Speaking of which, and invitations to tag along, will Miss Sek be joining us on the mission?"

Dorothy shook her head. "Unfortunately not. I don't look forward to spending that much time apart from her, but it's comforting to know the house will be left in her capable hands." She held up the journal. "May I take this?"

"Yes, I'm done with it all for the moment."

She held the book against her chest. The posture, combined with her unkempt hair and sloppy clothes, made her look like a student at the university. "I'll send Beatrice down when we've decided on a restaurant. Anything you'd care to suggest?"

"Whatever you choose should be fine."

"So noted." She tapped the journal. "Thank you for going to all this trouble."

Trafalgar gestured toward the ceiling. "You seemed to be otherwise occupied."

Dorothy smiled, her blush darkening the freckles across the bridge of her nose. "Quite. Be ready to leave in approximately an hour. Maybe ninety minutes."

"I will be ready."

Dorothy left and returned upstairs, while Trafalgar began putting away her maps. Dinner would be good, a nice way to mark the beginning of their journey and bid a temporary goodbye to both London and Beatrice.

INTERLUDE

THE CAFÉ wasn't doing much business at that time of evening, and Riya found herself the focus of an overzealous waitress who had nothing else to occupy her attention. She had arrived early for the rendezvous and couldn't do anything but wait. She nibbled on a biscuit, nursed her coffee, and read the news. At the agreed-upon time, her contact slid into the seat across from her. He reached out to grasp her cup, looked into it, and grimaced when he saw what it was.

"Coffee? In London?" He withdrew his hand, disgusted. "Whatever happened to 'when in Rome'?"

"I happen to prefer coffee to tea." She folded her newspaper and placed it to one side. "Besides, this ensures you don't steal my drink as soon as you arrive."

He smiled. "Diabolical."

Riya was already signaling the waitress, who approached to take the newcomer's order: lapsang souchong. Riya remained silent until the waitress had left the table.

"I've extended the offer to Lady Boone. She's presented it to the Society, and now they're all certainly debating the pros and cons of accepting."

"Where do you think they'll land?"

Riya said, "They'll agree. I'm positive."

The waitress brought his tea. He thanked her with a smile and took a sip. "Well, the money is being moved as we speak. The first installment will be available whenever they say yes."

"Good." She folded her hands around her coffee. "I don't like the time frame. They're unlikely to agree before leaving the country, which means we'll have to wait until they return."

"Exactly as it should be," he said. "Their experiences on this mission will make them receptive to what we have to say. It's why we chose to reach out now."

"I know. I just wish we could have worked with them from the beginning."

He shook his head. "A bad idea. If we had interfered in the formation of their partnership, we could have ruined everything. The butterfly effect, you know."

"Yes, I know." She looked out the window.

He let her stew in silence for a long moment. He savored his tea. "When will you be going back to 1922?"

"After lunch," Riya said. "I'll schedule my arrival so I can approach Dorothy as soon as they return from Brazil."

He hesitated with the teacup at his bottom lip. "She'll be vulnerable."

"I know. It can't be helped. Time is, ironically, of the essence. We need Trafalgar and Boone on our side as early as possible or all will be lost."

"Well, if anyone can marry haste with compassion, it's you."

She arched an eyebrow. "That almost sounded like a compliment."

He winked and relaxed in his seat to finish his tea.

Riya lifted her coffee and took a long drink. It was almost cool enough that it wouldn't burn her tongue, but she didn't mind a bit of a burn. She needed the caffeine to bolster her confidence before she went back to the office for her next trip.

Traveling in time was a wearisome affair even when one wasn't stressed about the end of the world.

CHAPTER FOUR

THERE WAS a point when land was no longer visible and water stretched out in every direction. Trafalgar made sure she was on-deck when it happened. She rested her hands on the railing and held her breath as the last vestige of solid ground disappeared like a mirage. The ship beneath her feet suddenly felt just a little less solid and her fingers curled around the cold metal. She kept her head up and her eyes open, took a series of measured breaths, and eventually managed to loosen her grip.

She had mentioned her unease about ocean travel when Dorothy revealed that was how they would be making the journey. Dorothy kindly offered to make arrangements for an airship instead, but Trafalgar insisted her anxiety wasn't worth the time they would lose. She appreciated the gesture but her fear of the sea was something she needed to get over. Dorothy bought passage on a luxury ship in an effort to make Trafalgar as comfortable as possible, and so far it had been working.

Until now, when land was out of sight.

It seemed impossible to be on a body of water so vast that land was nowhere to be seen. If the ship went down, rescue was at least one curve of the planet away.

She caught herself trembling. She clenched her hands until they were still, then pushed away from the railing. It would do no good staring at the horizon now. She would distract herself with work. She had been brushing up on her Portuguese in anticipation of their journey. Neville and other explorers had also chronicled the languages of several tribes who lived in the area, and Trafalgar was trying to learn as much of that as possible, just in case. She was nowhere near conversant in any of the languages but she was confident she could manage in an emergency.

Cora had also sequestered herself. The linguist had been silent on the trip to the docks and kept to herself once they were finally at sea. Trafalgar didn't know the exact details of what led to Cora's self-detention in the Wraysbury mental hospital, other than several young women met their deaths, but she knew Cora blamed herself. Dorothy trusted Cora on the mission and her faith was enough for Trafalgar, but she would nevertheless keep an eye on the woman until she had proven herself.

Dorothy, meanwhile, had been in her cabin since they left London. At a guess, Trafalgar had to say it was depression due to Beatrice staying behind. Ordinarily that wouldn't have been an issue. Dorothy would have found someone on the ship - another passenger, a crew member, a waitress in the dining room - and taken her as a "traveling companion." This time she was focused on Neville's journals and maps of the areas he had already traveled.

Trafalgar knew it was a good thing to have a partner who was focused on work, on planning what steps should be taken before they arrived, but it was so out of character that she couldn't help but worry. She seemed to have come to terms with Desmond's passing, but Trafalgar knew all too well how grief could find the smallest cracks in which to hide. She decided to give Dorothy her space while they were at sea but also check in on her from time to time, just to make sure she was truly coping well.

Trafalgar thought her own cabin was lovely, if a bit cramped. She had received an outer room, so she was able to open the porthole to let in the chilly sea air. Dorothy had ensured there wouldn't be any nonsense about denying her an upper-level room due to the color of her skin. Trafalgar was both touched and annoyed by the kindness. She obviously wished it wasn't necessary and she much preferred those instances when Dorothy forgot it would be an issue. Still, she was doing it to ensure Trafalgar was treated with fairness, so she chose to be grateful.

Her room reminded her of a train berth. Every inch was utilized and there was barely much space to stretch. She wondered how married couples or those traveling with children could bear it. One bed against one wall and a writing table opposite. There was a wash basin underneath the porthole with a small mirror, which she angled so she could see her reflection. Her hair, long and satin, fell across her shoulder like a sash.

Before departing, she and Dorothy had met with a contact named Ignacio Mata. He was visiting England from his native Barcelona and Dorothy decided to make an appointment to see if his unique curse could help them on the upcoming expedition. Ignacio had once found a djinn and wished to know the future. His wish was granted: he had memories of the future the way most people remembered the past. Hazy and sometimes imprecise, but definitely useful. They had only met him once before, but in his mind they were old acquaintances.

He had greeted them warmly. Once they were settled, Dorothy said, "On our last expedition, we required a very sturdy box. Metal, nigh-indestructible."

He'd arched an eyebrow. "And what supplies should be inside of it?"

"It doesn't matter. The standard supplies. Ropes, ammunition, a first-aid kit. Enough for it to be clear that the box isn't empty, but we don't require anything specific."

"My, my, very intriguing."

Trafalgar had smiled. The box had been instrumental in saving Dorothy from dying inside an ancient security system. But if Dorothy wasn't going to bring up the details, then she didn't want to be the one to ruin the mystery. She'd asked Ignacio what he'd brought for this mission, and his face fell. He drummed his fingers on the arm of his chair before he answered.

"You never give me much information. Probably so I won't warn you or give you information about your futures. So I don't know the specifics." He had opened his satchel and held up a small bag. "Painkillers. Very potent, only barely on this side of legal. You... you asked for quite a lot of them."

Dorothy had glanced at Trafalgar before taking the bag. "Thank you. I'm certain it will make all the difference. After all, the three of us are meant to have a very long relationship, isn't that right?"

"As far as I know," Ignacio said. "Please do not make my memory a liar."

When he was getting ready to leave, Trafalgar noticed his gaze kept drifting to her. She finally called him on it. "Is there something you wish to tell me, Señor Mata?"

"There is nothing to tell," he insisted. "I just... I'm..." She straightened his posture and smiled, one hand against his chest. "I merely wished to say how lovely your hair looks."

"My hair?"

"Mm-hmm." He was moving toward the door as he made the noise, bidding them farewell. Though it was only their second meeting, she already noted that he always seemed very eager to leave after their company. Most likely he was anxious about letting some future information slip if he allowed himself to engage in casual conversation.

Now, aboard the ship taking them to Brazil, she examined her hair in the mirror and wondered what had drawn his attention. Was she going to cut it? Change the style? The idea of a fresh look had been swirling at the back of her mind for a few weeks. She thought about cutting it to commemorate Desmond's death, but she didn't want to infringe on Dorothy's grief. He was a good man, kind and brave, but the truth was they had barely known one another.

Still, her hair was very long. It was a very... British affectation. She thought of her mother and the women of her village, the home from which she had been so cruelly stolen. They were bald because it was easier, and women had better things to do than primp and wash and braid themselves all morning. In her memory, it was the men wore their hair long, the warriors who ceremoniously braided their hair before hunting or battle. The mane of a lion and the sleek lines of his mate...

Trafalgar opened the drawer next to her bed and found a set of grooming supplies. Ignacio could merely have been complimenting her hair. Hell, he might even have been flirting. She took a moment to consider what she was about to do. It was a very drastic step to take based on how a man looked at her. But that wasn't her true motivation, was it? It had merely opened her eyes to a truth she'd been ignoring. She missed her home. She had been so young when she was taken that she doubted she could find her way back, but there was something she could do to honor the place of her birth.

She withdrew the scissors and went back to the mirror.

Dorothy was smiling when she opened the door, but her expression went through a quick succession of emotions once she saw her guest. She knew it would be Trafalgar but she hadn't anticipated such a drastic change in the other woman's appearance. Trafalgar grinned and dipped her chin, tilting her head to one side to prove the new look was indeed as complete as it appeared. Her head was completely shaved, a smooth dome that shone in the light coming from the porthole behind Dorothy.

"My goodness," Dorothy said. "You look amazing."

"Thank you, Lady Boone," Trafalgar said. "I must confess I was a bit worried you would be scandalized."

Dorothy gestured her inside. "Me? Heavens, have you met me? It will take more than a haircut to drive me to the fainting couch. Although I must say that I hope you have a sizable collection of hats once winter arrives. London can be unforgiving to the bald."

"I'll have to shop for some." She entered the room and noted the tidy bed, the cluttered desk. "I haven't been to see Cora yet. Do you think she'll be appalled?"

"She's spent more time in Africa than anyone else in the Society." Dorothy reclined against the desk, arms crossed over her chest. "I may know you better, but she knows the culture. Unless this is merely your way of coping with the fact we're at sea."

Trafalgar smiled. "No. It's a decision that has been a long time coming. Since you brought it up, I'm doing fine with the ocean." She glanced at the porthole and moved to take a seat on Dorothy's bed. "I'm a bit uneasy that we can no longer see land, but perhaps I won't notice as much if I remain below decks."

Dorothy said, "And it's no different than being on an airship above heavy cloud cover."

"That actually helps. Thank you."

Dorothy dipped her head in acknowledgement, then gestured at the desk. "As you can see, I've spent the majority of the trip going over these journals. Neville is quite a character, don't you think?"

"Very excitable." Trafalgar smiled. "He was so careful and studious until he reached the jungle, and then he became like a schoolboy."

"Yes, exactly!" Dorothy laughed. "I respect a man who finds joy in his work. It doesn't all have to be stuffiness and weighty words. Desmond truly appreciates being in a strange, mysterious place."

Trafalgar tensed slightly. "You mean Neville."

"Of course."

"You said Desmond."

"No, I..." She stopped herself before the lie was fully formed. Her shoulders sagged and she moved to sit beside Trafalgar on the bed. "Crumbs. Yes, I do see something of Desmond in Captain Neville. Perhaps I'm merely projecting my own unsettled thoughts onto his writing."

Trafalgar said, "No, I had the same thoughts when I went through the journals. I didn't want to say anything for fear of unnecessarily invoking them."

Dorothy sighed. "I suppose racing to Neville's rescue is my way to karmically make amends for the fact I couldn't save Des. I promise I won't allow it to interfere with my common sense. If you think it is at any point, you have my permission to give me a swift kick."

"Literally?"

"Figuratively."

Trafalgar clicked her tongue in disappointment. Dorothy shoved her shoulder, and they both laughed. Dorothy draped one leg over the other and rested her hands on them.

"I admit, I'm a bit more lonely than I expected."

"That's never been an issue for you," Trafalgar said. "Even on missions where Beatrice remained home, you had no problem finding companionship. If the other passengers aren't receptive, perhaps Miss Hyde would be amenable to your company."

Dorothy said, "It's not a lack of interest. Except on Cora's part... she's actually only interested in men, as boring as that sounds. But I haven't pursued anyone. To be honest, I... I'm not interested in dalliances. I'm confident I could find someone willing to share my berth if I put a bit of efforts into it. But despite that and despite knowing Beatrice doesn't mind the fact I occasionally wander, I can't bring myself to want to. Even though I'm lonely."

"You're lonely for *her*. That's not a weakness."

"Well, it's certainly not a strength. It's awfully awkward, to be quite honest."

Trafalgar smiled. "You're maturing. You want to settle down."

Dorothy sneered.

"Or," Trafalgar corrected, "you've discovered that of all the women in the world, there is only one beguiling enough to be worth your time and strong enough to keep up with you no matter where you may end up."

Dorothy nodded slowly. "That I believe I could accept. Thank you, Trafalgar."

"My pleasure." She stood. "With that, I shall leave you to... however you decide to spend your time. I noticed you haven't been to bed yet."

"We've only been at sea for a few hours."

"Yes, and it was a very early morning for us both. You deserve a nap, Lady Boone. It will be a few days before we arrive. You should take the time to relax."

Dorothy said, "I think I'll take your advice. And I may even follow your lead." She reached up and touched her red curls. "It would save me so much time in the mornings..."

"No," Trafalgar said without hesitation. "You would look atrocious without hair."

Dorothy swung her foot at Trafalgar, who deftly avoided the kick by dancing closer to the door. She waved over her shoulder as she fled the room, shutting the door behind her before Dorothy could launch a second attack.

CHAPTER FIVE

CORA HYDE didn't sleep for the first three days of their journey. She wasn't surprised by that fact, and had actually expected her anxiety to be far worse. Sleep had been elusive since her disastrous final mission to Khirokitia. The darkness of closed eyes reminded her of those caverns deep beneath the surface of the world where she'd lost three young women. Ada, Martha, Nellie. A bloody rope was enough evidence to deduce what happened to Ada, but the other two... gone with no trace, vanished because she lacked the courage to go back into the dark to find them.

Logically, she knew that going back into the caves would only have resulted in her own demise. That knowledge did nothing to assuage her guilt. The girls had been so very young and excited at the opportunity to join her in the field. Mere students whose parents couldn't even bury remains because no one was capable of venturing back to retrieve whatever might have been left behind.

Her stay at Wraysbury Hospital had done wonders to raise her spirits from suicidal to mere depression. She could function. She could dress, fix her hair, put on a good enough performance to stop her friends from looking at her like she was fragile. The pain was still there, but it was manageable. Once the haze lifted, she realized Dorothy Boone was the one person who never treated her as broken or looked at her with pity. That was why Cora chose to come along on this mission. She believed herself ready but, just in case she wasn't, Dorothy was the one person she trusted to not think less of her, and to pick up her slack if necessary.

When she finally emerged from her room on the fourth day, she found

Dorothy and Trafalgar in the ship's grand dining room. They were seated close enough to the bank of windows to see the ocean, but not so close to suffer from a chill. There were already plates in front of both of them, but they seemed to be closer to the beginning of their meal than the end.

Trafalgar gestured for her to join them and Cora apologized for cloistering herself. Dorothy waved off the apology.

"You've been under tremendous strain. Choosing to come along with us was a big step. Take as much time as you need to process what it means." She gestured at the seat across from her. "The waiter should be back in a moment if you're hungry."

"Thank you. I'm famished." She took in Trafalgar's shaven pate as she sat down. "A bold new look, Miss Trafalgar. It's incredibly striking."

Trafalgar smiled. "Thank you. I was inspired to commemorate the start of this expedition."

"Not to mention we'll be deep inside a tropical rainforest," Cora said. "I'm certain Dorothy and I will be envying your lack of hair by noon on the first day." The waiter appeared as promised, and Cora put in an order for an extremely modest breakfast. When he was gone, Cora faced her friends again. "What have I missed? I assume the two of you haven't been resting on your laurels this whole time."

"Hardly." Dorothy sipped her tea. "We've determined the name of the guides Captain Neville's men used from his earliest correspondence. Our first order of business upon arriving in Belém will be finding those guides and learning more of what happened once Neville entered the jungle." She speared a piece of her egg and brought it to her mouth, then paused before taking her bite. "Now there is a slightly uncomfortable topic that must be brought up before the mission gets underway."

Cora smiled knowingly. "The fact that you and Trafalgar are in charge and I am merely a glorified assistant?"

Dorothy's smile was bashful. "I apologize. I certainly don't think of you as my subordinate in any way. But~"

"But in situations such as the one we're about to embark upon, it's necessary to have a clear chain of command. I haven't been in the field lately, so it only makes sense that I defer to you."

Dorothy visibly relaxed. "I'm glad we've gotten that taken care of. The last thing we need is a miscommunication in the jungle." She scanned the room and lifted her hand to summon the waitress. "Now our only order of business for the rest of the trip is simply to enjoy ourselves. Sleeping in comfortable beds, eating wonderfully catered meals, wearing freshly-laundered clothes. I don't know how long we'll be away from civilization, but I have little doubt we'll soon be missing luxuries like this. Let's not take it for granted."

Trafalgar lifted her glass of juice, and Cora lifted her drink to tap it in a toast. Dorothy did the same, then moved the glass so she could get a refill from the just-arrived waitress.

"To the comforts of modern life," Dorothy said.

"And to roughing it," Cora added, "and coming out stronger the other side."

Dorothy nodded her approval and they all three took a drink. They had two more days left on the ship, and Cora was determined not to waste another second hiding in her cabin.

The ship arrived in Brazil on schedule. Dorothy took Trafalgar onto the deck as they pulled into the harbor so she could point out Neville's ship, the *Herald*, still awaiting the return of its crew. It had been stuck there for a year, most likely a bane to the dockmasters, and she could only hope it wasn't forced to remain there much longer.

Most people in London likely thought of South America as a completely wild and uncivilized place, as Dorothy herself had believed until she began planning this trip. But the port city of Belém was a booming metropolis, still flourishing from the rubber trade which had injected the modern world into this most remote of places. Developers had struggled to turn this place into a place of profit, even laying a railroad through the wilderness. The reports she read indicated nature had fought to reclaim its dominion at every turn, but eventually Man won out, as it tended to do with depressing regularity.

Dorothy was among the first people off the ship, stopping after she stepped off the gangplank to acclimate to solid ground. She put on her sunglasses to examine the buildings near the harbor. Cora put a hand on Trafalgar's elbow to steady herself.

"Are you all right?"

Cora smiled self-consciously. "Land legs. I forgot what it was like to spend most of a week on a ship and then return to land."

"Your mind needs a moment to catch up with your body." Trafalgar patted Cora's hand, adjusting her posture so they looked like friends linking arms instead of one person providing support for another. "Take as much time as you need."

Dorothy stood a few paces ahead of them. The majority of their luggage was scheduled to be delivered to their hotel, but she'd kept the heavy leather bag containing Neville's journals. She took out one that she'd perused on the ship and flipped it open to a hand-drawn map of the town. The captain had helpfully only written the names of the necessary landmarks - docks, market, hotels - and it didn't take long to get her bearings. The town stretched to the south, following the jagged coastline, and their destination was due east of the docks. She looked back to make sure her companions were ready before she gestured to the road.

"We'll most likely find our guides close to the edge of town. Shall we walk or take a tram?"

"I think walking would serve us best in terms of reclaiming our equilibrium," Cora said. "If Miss Trafalgar is kind enough to provide her arm for a bit longer."

Trafalgar smiled and patted Cora's hand. "For as long as you need."

Dorothy touched the brim of her hat to them. She led their trio through the bustling streets. Trafalgar's head drew a handful of curious looks, but no one in the group commented on the attention she was receiving. They paused only long enough for Dorothy to buy bananas, one for each of them, which they ate as they followed the rudimentary map through the narrow streets of Old City to a small brick building with a large window looking out at traffic like the eye of a cyclops. Dorothy squinted at the jumble of words painted on the glass.

"My Portuguese is rustier than I'd like to admit, but I think this is the place."

Cora had long ago found her stability, so she released Trafalgar's arm to follow her and Dorothy inside. The shop's front room was a welcome respite from the humidity. Dorothy removed her hat and used it to fan her face as her eyes acclimated to the darkness. She moved to stand closer to the circulation of a ceiling fan, which teased her hair away from her face. Cora ventured even further and craned her neck to look up a flight of stairs to the second floor.

"Hello?"

"*Olá*, hello!" The man's voice echoed from somewhere to their right. A few moments later a door opened and he stepped into view. His black hair was shaggy and unkempt, but the bushy mustache covering his upper lip was meticulously groomed. He wore a faded pink shirt unbuttoned enough to reveal the tank top underneath. He held out large hands and smiled at them.

"Americans?"

"British," Dorothy corrected.

"Even better. God save the Queen, and all that." His speech was suddenly colored by a British accent, thought Dorothy couldn't say for certain whether that had changed after his first brief words. "My name is Marco Eiriz, you can call me Eiriz. It's a much more interesting name." He moved to the desk in the corner and cleared off a precarious stack of maps. "How may I help you ladies?"

"My name is Dorothy Boone. This is Trafalgar, and the woman by the stairs is Cora Hyde. We'd like to employ you as our guide."

He sat down and nodded. "You'll do no better than me, my friends. My family has called this city home for over seventy years. I know it like the back of my hand. Old and new, I can show you the best we have to offer."

Dorothy said, "I'm certain you could. But I meant we need you to be our guide into the forest."

For the first time, his expression wavered. "An expedition? Where..."

He looked toward the door. "How many will be in your party?"

"Just us."

"Just the three of you. You three... ladies."

Trafalgar said, "We're quite capable of handling ourselves in extreme situations."

"I'm sure you are, miss." He stood again. "This isn't a matter of... look... I've taken a half dozen groups into the jungle. There are obstacles you're most likely unaware of. It's not just the heat and the wildlife. Although the heat and the wildlife are both enough by themselves to dissuade you. The wasps alone..." He shuddered at some memory. "No matter how clear a path may seem, you will require a machete to hack through vines that hang in your way. I've seen men collapse from exhaustion, too weak to lift their arms to wipe away their tears."

"Then I suppose we will need to hire a few of your friends to provide the grunt work."

Eiriz sighed and put his hands on his hips. "They won't be cheap."

Dorothy said, "And I am not poor. We're not flighty women off on a lark, Mr. Eiriz. We are here on behalf of the Royal Geographical Society in an attempt to discover the fate of Captain Neville and the men of his expedition."

Eiriz stood up straighter. His face betrayed no emotion, but that was enough to give Dorothy a clue of his inner turmoil.

"Neville?" he said.

"That's correct." Dorothy held up the journal. "We know that he came here and hired you. His correspondence mentions you by name, Mr. Eiriz. Of course we'll pay you the going rate for your services. All we ask is that you show us where Neville was heading the last time you saw him."

"I can do better than that, Miss Boone." Eiriz's entire body sagged, as if he had just released some tension within himself. "I can take you to where we buried them."

CHAPTER SIX

WHILE EIRIZ gathered a small group of men to accompany them into the jungle, Dorothy took Trafalgar and Cora aside to discuss whether their mission had come to an unexpectedly sudden end. "It's not the outcome we were hoping for," she whispered, "but the potential for this was always there. We could get Mr. Eiriz to explain the circumstances and take that story back to London."

Cora said, "Certainly some of the men have families. They deserve to know their fathers or brothers or sons are resting somewhere more dignified than some unmarked grave in the middle of uncharted wilderness. I'm aware that I am the most fragile of our group, but I elect that we continue onward. If we cannot bring back their bodies, the least we can do is pay our respects at the site."

"I agree."

"We have a consensus, then."

Trafalgar looked toward Eiriz and Dorothy followed her gaze. He was seated with his elbows on the desk, one hand covering the lower half of his face. His good humor had faded, and he seemed to be genuinely haunted by what he'd revealed. Dorothy walked closer and he straightened a little, though his shoulders remained slumped.

"I spoke to the men, and they're supplying the boat. We'll be ready to leave within the hour. It shouldn't take us long to reach the site."

Dorothy said, "Perhaps we should head to the docks now, so we can depart immediately as soon as it's ready."

"Of course, yes." He stood up and pulled a bag from beneath his desk.

He opened a drawer and began transferring things to it. "While we're waiting, I can... I can try to explain what happened to your colleagues. The little of it that I actually understand."

"That would be greatly appreciated, Mr. Eiriz."

A touch of his previous showmanship seeped back into his face. "It's just Eiriz, *por favor*. 'Mister' is too formal. Stuffy." He slung the bag over his shoulder and stepped around the desk to lead the way out of the building.

Eiriz told the story over his shoulder as they traveled through town, only slightly out of breath despite the pace he set. Trafalgar had no trouble keeping up with him, but Dorothy and Cora both brought up the rear despite the fact they were all but jogging so they wouldn't be left behind.

"Captain Neville enlisted us to take him and a few of his men into the jungle. You know their mission, I assume? Discover the Pratear?"

Trafalgar was still keeping pace with him. "Yes. According to the journals, Neville believed he was close to locking in its location."

Eiriz nodded. "He was very excited, yes. People in this part of the world have spoken about the river for hundreds of years. It was believed any item washed in its waters became solid silver. There have even been a great number of disreputable markets for items supposedly created in the Pratear. Those items are all counterfeit, of course, mostly silver-plated rather than as advertised. Most educated people accept the river is a myth."

Dorothy was breathing hard now. "But a myth you're happy to promote if it helps tourism."

He looked sheepishly back at her. "Of course we're very remorseful about the loss of life. We attempted to dissuade Captain Neville from venturing into the forest, but he insisted."

"We don't blame you for what happened, Eiriz," Trafalgar said. "In our line of work, death is always a possibility. Please, continue."

"Captain Neville paid us all very handsomely for three days. We hired a boat. We took him and his men upriver. One man on his team kept a very close eye on the map and eventually told us where to drop anchor. They told us we could remain with the boat while they ventured overland. I warned them it would be a treacherous journey, but Neville was insistent. So we let them go and stayed with the boat. Three days, since that was all he paid us for."

"Neville and his team never returned?"

"We never saw them alive again, Miss Hyde. I couldn't just abandon them, so I went to see if I could pick up their trail. I found them not far from the river." He grimaced. "Their remains... I found their remains. We hadn't heard a sound the entire time we were waiting, but the men had been slaughtered. I thought the best course of action would be to give them a proper burial and take my men back to safety."

They were close enough to the docks that Dorothy could see a group of men loading supplies onto a boat she assumed was theirs. Several of them were bare-chested, and she saw a gallery's worth of tattoo art on every available stretch of skin.

"Why didn't you alert the authorities?" Trafalgar asked.

Dorothy answered before Eiriz could summon the courage to confess. "He was afraid. I assume yours is not the most reputable company offering guides excursions into the forest. From the looks of it, you hire men based on their strength and courage. These men most likely have criminal records. If you went to the authorities and revealed Captain Neville and his entire team had died under mysterious circumstances, you would have been held responsible."

Eiriz stopped running and faced them. "You have to understand--"

"We do." Dorothy's forehead was now dotted with sweat. She took off her hat, wiped away the shine, and fanned her face with the fedora's brim. "You were in a difficult situation. My only real question is why Neville would choose a company as questionable as yours. He had the full support of the RGS behind him. He could have afforded anybody, so why did he go to you? No offense."

"None taken, obviously," Eiriz said. "Even if there was, I've remained silent for far too long to take the high road in this situation." He gestured at the boat. "It's far past time that I make amends."

Dorothy said, "I heartily agree. Please, lead the way."

He continued on. Trafalgar and Cora moved closer to Dorothy before following.

"What do you think?" Trafalgar asked under her breath.

"He seems sincere," Dorothy said, "but given what he's just confessed, we would be fools to completely trust him or his cohorts. There's every possibility that they robbed Captain Neville and his men, killed them, and now they're taking us into the forest to do the exact same thing."

"Odds?" Trafalgar asked.

Dorothy pondered for a moment. "Sixty percent chance he's telling the truth. What do you say?"

"I would agree with that assessment."

Cora said, "Forty percent chance of being murdered if we get on the boat. Not enough to make me turn back, but I'll definitely not be turning my back on him once we're underway."

Trafalgar checked the time. "Despite Eiriz's assurances that we don't have far to go, there's a very real chance we'll be spending the night on this boat. I'll go ahead and suggest now that we sleep in shifts."

Dorothy smiled and led the way up the ramp. "Who can sleep? We're about to travel into a mysterious jungle with a group of pirates and thieves in search of men who died in search of a river of silver. I may not sleep for a solid week after this."

The river was sluggish and red-brown, bracketed on either side by surprisingly lush foliage. Dorothy took pictures of trees, angling her head back to look up into the canopy, and tried to track the sounds she heard back to actual animals. Eiriz caught her squinting between the trees. "For every beast you hear," he told her, "there are ten closer to you that you will never know about." His eyes darted about for a moment and he pointed at the water. "There."

Dorothy followed his finger. At first all she saw was the ripples caused by the wake of the boat. Then there was a lump, something pressing upward without actually breaking the surface tension, followed by a rapid wrinkling as whatever it was swam away.

"Remarkable. Eel?"

He shrugged. "We shall never know."

Trafalgar's worry that the day was growing late had quickly become a reality. The river was naturally darker than the city, but it was clear that the sun was rapidly sinking.

"How much farther to our destination?"

Eiriz said, "Not far. We will arrive there near dusk. We can anchor the boat there since it's dangerous to sail at night, but we can use the time to trek to the burial site."

Dorothy said, "So you expect us to follow you into the forest, on our own, at night, to find the bodies of the men you claim were killed through unknown circumstances?"

"You are the ones who hired me, Miss Boone," he said, "but you would be foolish not to have some concern at this situation. But I promise you have nothing to worry about. I would promise the men who accompany us into the forest will be unarmed, but they cannot make much progress without machetes. And I would offer to let you carry firearms if you were proficient."

Dorothy's laugh echoed off the water. "Proficient? Do you happen to have a gun on you?"

He straightened and took a revolver from the back of his belt. She took it from him with a head-tilt of thanks, turned, and sighted a plump yellow-brown fruit hanging from a tree on the banks. She aimed without hesitation and fired. The fruit exploded in a pulpy mess and the foliage shuddered with the retreat of frightened animals. The deck shook as Eiriz's men came running to see what was happening.

Eiriz calmed them down by shouting something in Portuguese, then faced Dorothy again. She held out the gun to him, but he gestured for her to keep it.

"Are your friends as good with a gun as you are?" he asked in English.

"Cora is as good as me. Trafalgar is better, I believe."

"Then you shall all be armed when we leave the boat. Both for your own peace of mind and any local fauna that might think we look tasty."

"I believe that is a deal we can agree to." She looked past him at the men. "Would you kindly apologize to them for the disruption?"

Eiriz said, "I don't believe I will do that. Men like this, on a boat alone with three women... ah. Well, I will only say that perhaps it is better if they are a little scared of you."

Dorothy smiled. "Wise."

She slipped the gun into her belt, watching the men from the corner of her eye as she turned. It would be bad if they decided she was a threat, but a little wariness could be a good defense against any of them deciding to take liberties.

Night had fallen when the boat drifted closer to shore. Eiriz dropped anchor while his men filled a lantern and checked the sharpness of their machetes. Dorothy, Trafalgar, and Cora had changed into outfits more suitable for trekking through the Amazon. The weight of the boots, the thickness of her blouse and trousers, and the bulkiness of the vest made Dorothy feel as though she was wearing a suit of armor in anticipation of fighting a dragon. Protection came at the expense of comfort, as the new garb also made the night feel at least five degrees hotter.

Eiriz stopped them before they disembarked. He had totally abandoned his laidback demeanor from the office and now seemed more like a soldier.

"We'll have four men in front, clearing the way. I'll be with them. You'll follow behind us. There will be two men bringing up the rear. All sorts of things may be attracted by our light. I expect you ladies to take care of those threats as they arise."

Trafalgar had chosen a shotgun and patted the stock. "We'll be ready."

"Then let's get out there so we can be quicker back."

"Shouldn't we take more lanterns?"

"Ideally," Eiriz said. "But we don't have enough hands available to carry more. The men will need both arms to cut away vegetation in some places."

Dorothy didn't like the idea of only having one light, but she couldn't fault his logic.

Eiriz left two men to watch the boat and then gestured for them to disembark. Their point man, the largest of the group with a complex set of tattoos marking his exposed arms, lifted his lantern and set out on a trail only he could see. Occasionally, one of the men behind him moved ahead to chop away a vine that was as thick as Dorothy's waist, clearing the way for them to continue onward. Eiriz was directly ahead of Dorothy, and even in the paltry light she could see the sweat gathering in dark patches on his shirt. He was mostly a dark shape limned with light from their leader's lantern.

"It's been a year since you brought Neville and his team out here," she said. "How can you be so certain you remember the exact location?"

One of the men behind her answered in Spanish. Eiriz barked something at him in the same language, then grumbled something else in Portuguese as he ducked under a branch.

"It was the last time I came out here," he admitted. "After what I saw... those bodies..." Dorothy saw him shudder. "It's not something you quickly forget, *senhorita*. Believe me, I have been trying."

Mention of his trauma made Dorothy turn to check on Cora. Her friend swatted at something invisible that Dorothy heard buzzing as it zipped away. She looked cautious but no more than their current situation warranted. She noticed Dorothy's scrutiny and offered her a smile.

"I was hoping the mosquitos would be asleep at this late hour."

"That would seem to be the main benefit of doing this after dark."

Eiriz said, "The other benefit is getting it over with as quickly as possible. I want to be done with this. Perhaps putting these men to rest properly will ease my conscience."

"One can only hope," Dorothy said. "If it truly is as you told us, you have nothing to feel guilty about. Captain Neville was going to come out here whether you brought him or not."

"But it was unlikely he would find anyone else to bring him," Eiriz said. "Perhaps if I had refused, he would have been forced to go home."

Dorothy smiled even though she knew he couldn't see it. "You haven't met many British men, have you? Especially those who believe they are about to become famous. Neville would have been on this path no matter what you said. Just as the three of us would be."

Eiriz dipped his head and turned away. "We're nearly there, I believe."

Trafalgar moved closer to Dorothy. When she spoke, her voice was so low that Dorothy could barely make out the words. "How many men are supposed to be bringing up the rear of our party?"

Dorothy tensed at the question. She matched Trafalgar's volume. "Two. Why?"

"Because when we left, it sounded like two. Then, a moment ago, I couldn't hear anyone behind us. Now I can distinctly hear three people moving through the underbrush."

Dorothy tried to listen, but she could only hear leaves being mulched under their boots and mud squelching as they high-stepped out of the deeper puddles. She certainly couldn't tell how many people there were in the group, but she trusted Trafalgar's assessment.

"What's your suggestion?"

"Let Cora pass you. I'll bring up the rear so that I'm their next target."

Dorothy said, "Offering yourself as bait?"

"Is there anyone else you would elect in my place?"

"Well.. I suppose I should at least symbolically offer to be the decoy."

Trafalgar chuckled. "I won't go quietly."

"I'm sure you won't."

Trafalgar fell back. A moment later, Cora came up alongside Dorothy.

"Something's afoot, isn't it?"

"Nothing to be concerned about," Dorothy said. "Trafalgar has it under control."

Cora pressed her lips together. "I don't have to be coddled."

"No one is coddling you, dear. Trafalgar is our best fighter. And, in a pinch, I can fight better than you. We're simply stacking the deck in our favor. It will be your job to protect Eiriz and his men."

"Be careful," Cora said.

"Always. Tell Eiriz what's happening, but be discreet. We don't know how his hired goons will react to a threat."

Cora nodded. She touched Dorothy's arm as she moved forward. Dorothy glanced back. The lantern's light illuminated Trafalgar in a dim halo but left most of the forest around her in shadow. Whoever was stalking them was being forced to do so in absolute darkness. She assumed it was tribesmen who knew this terrain like the backs of their hands. There was the possibility this was all a matter of trespassing where they didn't belong. A simple misunderstanding that, with time, she could—

A shout from one of Eiriz's men startled her. "Savages!" It was followed by a sound Dorothy identified as a knife sinking into wood, although she was certain the reality was something far more gruesome, and a shriek of pain. It sounded like an animal being slaughtered. She heard glass shatter as the lantern was dropped. Its fuel and flame spilled and hissed when it touched water, but flared where it caught on leaves or moss. The light intensified enough for Dorothy to see people between the gaps in the trees. Bare-chested, their skin smeared with river mud, eyes and mouths stark against the crusty masks. Three to her right, at least six converging on Eiriz and his men, and three behind Trafalgar. They had been flanked, surrounded, cut off from the boat.

"Crumbs," she muttered.

With the element of surprise gone, their stalkers attacked. The report of Trafalgar's shotgun sounded almost obscene given their surroundings, but she only managed two shots before the gun was knocked from her hands by a thick wooden club. Dorothy fired thrice at the men approaching her and managed to hit two of them. The last one put his hand over her face and shoved. She tripped over her feet and landed hard on her back. He loomed above her, a spear lifted with the stone tip aimed at her chest.

The top of his head erupted in a flood of red. Dorothy flinched and looked in the direction the shot had come from, but Cora was already lining up her next target. Dorothy let out the breath she'd been holding and got back onto her feet. The flames had grown into a wide wall of flickering light which revealed the entire tableau. Behind Cora, she saw Eiriz clutching a bloody wound in his shoulder and fumbling with his own revolver. The rest of his men were nowhere to be seen. Dorothy spun to see if Trafalgar needed help. Her blood ran cold when she saw that the forest behind her was empty.

"Trafalgar!"

"Dorothy!" Cora shouted.

Before Dorothy could respond, something slammed into her back hard enough to knock her off her feet. Her forehead cracked against a tree trunk and she twisted so that she could land on her back. She was vaguely aware of the bark flaking off, aware that her teeth had snapped shut on impact but she'd managed not to bite off her tongue, and she knew that her forehead was bleeding when she landed in the mud like a scarecrow which had lost its support pole.

After that, however, she wasn't aware of much at all.

CHAPTER SEVEN

TRAFALGAR RETURNED to her senses slowly, brief bursts of awareness that never added up to a sum total of consciousness. She knew she was being moved and heard voices all around her. Mostly male, one female, the latter of which she recognized as Cora. They spoke mostly in Portuguese. Cora attempted to make herself understood with English and Spanish, pleading with the men to "be careful with her." She knew she was taken a great distance and put on something soft. At one point she opened her eyes and saw she was in a room with cloth walls, something sturdier than a tent but not permanent. The walls were darkened by vast shadows thrown by the foliage which apparently surrounded them. The only furniture in the space was her bed, a squat chair next to it, and a table against the far wall. The flaps were open wide with no one visible standing guard. That sight was comforting enough to let her slip back into unconsciousness.

Time passed. She knew the sun had risen, but not how long it had been up or if it had actually risen multiple times since the last time she was awake. The thing that finally pulled her out of the fog was the intensity of the heat breaking when someone pressed a cold, wet cloth against her brow and cheeks. The chilled water rolled down over her face and finally prompted her eyes to flutter open and focus on her caretaker.

Cora smiled and relief flooded her features. "There you are. We were starting to get concerned." She picked up a packet from her bag on the floor and offered it to Trafalgar with a cup of water. "Painkillers," she said. "I found a great deal of them in your pack. Good planning, that."

Trafalgar nodded and swallowed the pill. "How long..."

"Only a few hours," Cora said. "The attack happened last night. How much do you remember?"

Trafalgar searched her memory, letting her attention drift past Cora to the canvas of the tent wall behind her. "I remember the ambush. There were three of them behind us. They had taken out Eiriz's men who were bringing up the rear. Their plan was most likely to eliminate us quietly, one at a time."

"Thankfully you were paying attention."

"Hmm. I fought them off to the best of my ability. Shortly after the fire began, I started losing ground. Someone leveled the field by shooting one of my attackers."

"That was me."

Trafalgar found Cora's hand to give it a squeeze. "Thank you."

"I was doing what I could to give you and Dorothy the upper hand."

"Where is Dorothy? The last I saw, she was nearly overrun."

Cora looked away. "She's... she wasn't... I'm sorry, Trafalgar. I couldn't risk going back for her. If I had, I might have gotten captured as well, and you needed help, and—"

"It's all right," Trafalgar said.

Cora blinked, but tears still gathered in her eyes. "So much for my grand return to exploration. Once again, I've left someone behind."

"Dorothy would have done the same thing in your position. I'm surprised she wasn't shouting for you to leave her behind."

"She couldn't have," Cora said. "Last I saw, she was lying unconscious at the base of a tree. Those men were converging on her. I had to make a choice. I couldn't fight them all, so I... I grabbed you and ran. I ran again."

Trafalgar pushed herself up with some effort and put a hand on Cora's shoulder. "I hope you don't regret your choice. I certainly don't. If our positions had been reversed, I'm sure Dorothy would have left me behind. I would have wanted her to. Two escaping capture is better than everyone being lost." She furrowed her brow and looked toward the tent opening. "We did escape capture, correct? Where are we? Whose camp is this?"

Cora wiped at her cheeks. "I was waiting for the right moment to tell you." She got off the bed, which Trafalgar could now see was a cot. It was low to the ground, and the canvas strained against its metal skeleton as she shifted her weight. Cora opened the tent flap and motioned someone to join them. "Eiriz and I managed to get away, but we were running blindly. Literally and figuratively. You have no idea how dark a forest can get. The fire behind us and the moon above provided a little light, but we quickly escaped its reach. I was certain we would never find our way back to the river, let alone civilization."

"But you managed to find someone?"

"Someone managed to find us," Cora said.

As if he'd been waiting for his cue, the tent flap opened and a man ducked inside. His skin was red and peeling from too much time in the sun. His hair was lighter than his beard for the same reason, but his eyes were bright and lively. He wore a lightweight shirt with the sleeves cut off above the elbows. He smiled when he saw she was awake, and he offered a hand.

"Miss Trafalgar." He had an unexpectedly posh British accent. "It's a delight to meet you at last. Your reputation in London made you out to be something of a legend, and Miss Hyde has spent the last few hours verifying them to be true."

"You're from London."

Cora said, "Indeed he is. Miss Trafalgar, allow me to introduce you to Captain Felix Neville of the *HMS Herald*."

Trafalgar blinked at him in surprise. Now she recognized him. In every photograph she'd seen of the missing captain, he had some sort of facial hair or another. This man was clean-shaven.

"You're alive."

Neville laughed. "Miss Hyde told me about the misconception. Not that I'm terribly surprised. I've been gone a very long time, and most of my men died in an ambush similar to the one you fell victim to. We had discovered the Pratear, and we were returning to the river when the tribe attacked. I was very badly injured. The people here found me. Tended my wounds, kept me alive. By the time I was stable enough to leave, my guides were long gone. I could have attempted finding my way back to Belém on my own, probably dying in the process, or I could stay here. Help my saviors and wait to see if anyone came looking for me."

"Putting our lives in danger in the process."

"I do apologize for that. The lives lost... I can never repay that debt. If there had been a way to send a message, to let anyone know where I was or the danger in coming after me, I would have sent it. But even after all the time I've spent here, I can't even begin to tell you exactly where 'here' is."

Trafalgar looked at Cora. "But you have some idea... right?"

Cora shook her head. "I know we're within walking distance of the river. But in which direction, and exactly how far, I haven't the foggiest."

"We're lost?"

Neville said, "The forest is a world unto itself. Even if you walked out of this village in the right direction and found a river, there's no way to be sure it's the same one that brought you in. There are hundreds of streams and branches and tributaries around here. Without a guide, you might just be walking yourselves in circles."

Trafalgar searched for a response to that, but nothing came to mind. "That's... not ideal..."

"I've been trying to map out the general area since I was well enough to move around. How long have I been here anyway?"

"About a year," Cora said.

He hmphed. "Feels much longer. Are you feeling up for a tour? Miss

Hyde has already been shown around. Met a few of the locals. They're very interested in meeting you as well."

Trafalgar pushed away the blankets. Cora obviously wanted to protest, but didn't manage to find the words before Trafalgar had already put her feet on the floor.

"I think it would help my recovery to get up and walk around. I'm feeling... my head is not quite..." She started to stand but only made it into a crouch before she collapsed back onto the bed.

Cora muttered, "Bloody hell, I was worried about this."

She saw Cora above her, and Neville leaning in with concern on his face, and then she saw nothing else.

Dorothy was seated in a chair. Cushioned, but uncomfortable. It was secured to the floor in some manner. Her wrists were strapped to the armrests. A firm-feeling strap stretched across her waist. Her feet were free, which would be good for kicking should the need arise, but she doubted she could get out of the chair without a good amount of assistance. Her head throbbed and she ached everywhere, which she took as a good sign that she wasn't paralyzed or missing any parts.

She was confident enough that she was alone to risk opening her eyes, though she kept her chin down. There was another chair in front of her, and one to either side. Her first thought was that she was in a theater, but that didn't make any sense. Lifting her head just a little, she could see more rows of chairs in front of her. There was no screen, but the seats were facing an oval wall with several smooth-edged holes that had once been doors or shelves. The ceiling was very low and curved. To her right was another empty hole that looked out on thick vegetation. A bug crawled up the wall, paused, and then vanished out through the window.

Sunlight flooded over the seats from behind her like a sheet, and she could hear birdsong. So whatever this place might be, it was open to the elements.

"Well," she whispered, just to break the silence and confirm she really was conscious.

Several minutes passed before she heard movement from behind her. She saw no reason to feign unconsciousness and turned her head to watch the man as he approached. He was darkly tanned, skinny to the point of emaciation, and his hair was cut close enough to his skull that his ears seemed to have been pasted to the side of a stone as a joke. He was bare-chested but wore a ragged pair of trousers caked to the knees with dry mud.

"Hello. Are the restraints too tight?"

"You're free to loosen them as much as you like."

He smiled and rested an elbow on the row of seats in front of her. His accent was American, which surprised her.

"I think we'll leave them as-is, if that's okay with you. What's your name?"

"Where are my friends?"

"What's your name?"

"Are they alive? Are you holding them prisoner as well?"

"You're not a prisoner." He seemed calm, unhurried. "What's your name?"

"What's *your* name?"

He put his hand against his chest. "Ketcham. What's yours?"

She considered lying or withholding the information, but saw no benefit to either tactic. "You may call me Lady Boone."

"Hah. We don't do titles very much here. Well, not all of us. We'll go with Boone, if that's okay with you. As for your friends, to the best of my knowledge, at least a few of them are still alive. I think most of the men were killed."

"And the women?"

"Ran off," he said. "One of them looked unconscious, but the others were carrying her. But this isn't exactly Piccadilly Circus, you know. Just because they were alive the last time I saw them doesn't mean they've survived until now."

Dorothy said, "How long has it been?"

"Most of a day. Why have you come?"

"We were looking for someone. An explorer who came into the forest a year ago and never came home."

"Rescue or recovery?"

"Ideally, we hoped it would be rescue. But we've since learned that it was more likely to be a recovery mission. Our guide told us the men we came to find had been killed. I assume it happened in an ambush like the one we suffered. Am I correct? Are your people responsible for their deaths?"

Ketcham shrugged. "Perhaps. Sometimes we have to dissuade trespassers."

Dorothy said, "So why did you save me?"

"That is an excellent question." He looked past her and Dorothy could hear someone else walking down the aisle toward them. "And I believe it's one best answered by our leader."

She twisted her neck again and saw a man she recognized despite the darkening of his skin and the lightening of his hair due spending too much time in the sun. His beard was thicker than it had been in the photographs she'd seen, but there was no doubting his identity.

"Captain Neville," she said. "You're alive."

"Indeed I am," he said. "And you came to rescue me?"

Dorothy was stunned and almost stuttered when she answered. "Yes, that's... that was the plan."

Neville sighed and looked at Ketcham. "That may prove more

complicated than you expected. Something has gone very wrong in this jungle, Lady Boone, and I fear I'm to blame. And if I'm not stopped, I fear I shall be the cause of a catastrophe so immense it could change the planet."

"Sorry," Dorothy said, "if you're not stopped…?"

He sighed. "I'm not the only Felix Neville in this forest, Lady Boone. One of us did something to cause widespread damage and one of us is trying to prevent it from spreading to the rest of the world."

"And which one are you?"

Neville looked hopeless. "All of this would be so much easier if I knew the answer to that question, my dear."

CHAPTER EIGHT

THE ACHES had only intensified when Trafalgar regained consciousness. She groaned and put a hand to her forehead. It was darker now, closer to nightfall, and she resigned herself to the knowledge she had lost an entire day. Cora appeared at her side again.

"Don't strain yourself," she said. "Captain Neville says you've probably contracted a bug. Now that you're awake, he can administer some medicine. It's most likely an infection from one of your wounds."

Trafalgar grunted and closed her eyes. "Has there been any sign of Dorothy?"

"I'm afraid not. To be honest, no one is looking. The forest is treacherous, and the attack on us is proof that the locals are out and causing trouble. The tribe hosting us is unwilling to risk their safety to look for Dorothy because they believe it's highly unlikely she survived the attack."

"This is Dorothy Boone we're talking about."

Cora said, "I know. But Felix has told me about the tribe who attacked us. They're vicious. They don't leave survivors. Maybe it would be best for him to explain everything himself. Things are very complicated here."

"Did he find the Pratear?"

"Yes," Cora said, but the way she averted her gaze indicated there was much more to the story. "Rest. There will be plenty of time to explain things later."

"You can explain it now," Trafalgar said. "I might as well get the information while I'm lying here doing nothing."

Cora said, "You're healing."

Trafalgar said, "When I am back on my feet, I won't have time to hear a long story about what's going on. Please, indulge me."

"Fine." Cora sighed. "We're in a village of the Urubi, the people who saved Felix. They call the people who attacked us children of the Burnt Empire."

"Ominous," Trafalgar said.

"You haven't heard the ominous part yet. According to the Urubi elders, the Burnt Empire didn't exist before a year ago. But the younger Urubi insist the Burnt Empire has been around for at least several centuries."

Trafalgar said, "The elders don't remember the other tribe? Perhaps a problem with their memories, or..."

"No," Cora said, "the ignorance is too widespread for that. They came to the conclusion that the Burnt Empire, along with all its history, came into existence all at once less than a year ago."

"You believe it's fabricated?"

Cora glanced toward the tent flap. "Felix explains it better. He believes something happened with time when he found the Pratear. He thinks the discovery caused something with affected the past in such a way that a new, aggressive tribe was created. It explains why his team was attacked on their way *out* of the forest rather than when they arrived. The Burnt Empire didn't exist at that point in time."

Trafalgar pushed herself up on her elbows, even though the movement made her head swim. "You believe he changed the course of history? That's impossible."

"He believes it. The Urubi believe it. And more importantly, the evidence seems to support his claim. Settlements exist. There is evidence of long-term habitation in areas where the elders claim there shouldn't be anything."

"So what's the explanation? Neville retroactively changed the course of history?"

Cora shrugged. "He's been a little cagey on that aspect of it, but it seems to be the case. He believes something he did or will do affects the past in a way that the present changed."

Trafalgar thought about that. If Ignacio could "remember" the future, perhaps time wasn't as linear as people liked to believe. And if that was true, any number of things could be possible.

"So what is his plan?"

"The Burnt Empire is savage. Cruel. Felix thinks that there is a way to fix what he changed, undo whatever caused them to be created, and return history to the way it was before he showed up. The alterative would be allowing them to run wild and dominate this entire area. The Urubi will most likely be the next victims if we let that happen."

Trafalgar raised an eyebrow. "It's 'we' now?"

Cora smiled shyly. "Captain Neville is quite charming. And he hasn't spent time with a woman from home for ages. He's a bit overbearing."

"Charming or overbearing, Miss Hyde," Trafalgar teased. "One or the other, or it will be clear that you're protesting too much."

"Oh hush." Cora checked Trafalgar's forehead and reached for the wet washcloth. "You're feverish. You don't know what you're saying."

Trafalgar smiled and allowed the sweat to be blotted from her skin. "You don't truly believe Lady Boone is dead, do you?"

Cora's hand paused. "I don't know. On the one hand, of course I hope she's alive. She's very resourceful... when she's uninjured and conscious. But that was not the case when last I saw her. And if she *is* still alive, then she's a prisoner of the Burnt Empire suffering unimaginable tortures. So if you want my honest opinion of what my hopes are, I don't think either option is preferable."

Trafalgar pressed her lips together and closed her eyes, unwilling to hope Dorothy had died quickly but equally unwilling to wish for her suffering. She reluctantly admitted Cora was right: for Dorothy Boone, there was simply no preferable outcome to their current situation.

"Mango?"

Dorothy looked up to see Captain Neville offering her a quartered globe, the pinkish flesh glistening in the dim sunlight washing through the hole behind her. She was famished but wary of accepting anything this man or any of his followers offered.

"It will be difficult to eat with my hands bound like this."

"I could feed you."

She made a face. "I believe I shall pass on that experience, thank you."

"Suit yourself." He took a bite and sat down in one of the chairs across the aisle from her. Dorothy found it peculiar that every chair in every row was facing the same direction. There was no space at the front of this narrow tube for a screen or a stage. Neville was chewing loudly, disgustingly, and Dorothy was about to snap at him when he spoke. "I'm aware of your reputation, Lady Boone. I know you have... a high moral standing. And I suppose if I want your help, I have to be more forthcoming. I have to tell you what's going on."

"That would be helpful. Untying me would also go a long way."

"When you know more, then I'll consider it." He took another bite of melon, and Dorothy regretted not taking it. "What do you suppose this is? This place where we've been holding you?"

"I haven't the foggiest," she admitted. "There are certain familiar aspects to the design, but on a whole, I'm stumped."

"This is an airplane."

She looked at him, then examined the space. A line of pill-shaped windows running along either side of the body. Rows of seats, clustered in groups of three, all facing forward.

"I've been in airplanes," she said. "None of them looked anything like this."

"You've been in planes from this era," Neville said. "This is Ackon Air flight 372, originating in Dallas, Texas, on February 12, in the year 1973."

Dorothy stared at him. "What in the world are you talking about?"

He twisted in the seat to face her. His lips were glistening from the melon, which had also dripped into his beard. His eyes were wild.

"This plane is from the future, Lady Boone."

She looked around at the grime and rot that seemed to cover every surface. She didn't know what the thing was, but his story was too utterly incredible to believe. She remembered the Society's debate about con artists. To sell a lie, it needed to be believable. Something so very ridiculous had to be the truth because no one would be crazy enough to make it up. And yet, this was a step too far.

"You've gone mad."

Neville said, "I assure you, that could not be farther from the truth."

"You attack the people who came to bring you home, you hold me prisoner, you insist there's a second version of you running around, and now you're telling me this ancient ruin is actually from fifty years in the future? How would you react to hearing this story, Captain Neville?"

He dropped his head. "I suppose you make a valid point. Except for one point: we aren't the ones who attacked you. And there's a reason the plane looks like it's over a century old. Because it is."

She nodded slowly. "Captain... Felix. Please, I'm begging you. Release me. Together we can find my friends and we can leave this place behind. We can get you the help you so badly need when we're back in London."

He stood up and assumed the tone of an orator. "In 1973, a plane left the airport in Dallas, Texas, en route to São Paulo. It was going to be a twelve hour flight. Not long after they crossed into Brazilian airspace, they came across an anomaly. The captain adjusted course but there was no way to avoid it entirely. The starboard wing was sheared off. The crew did their best, but a bird can't fly with a single wing. They crashed. Right here. Ninety percent of the passengers survived. Not a bad ratio, considering the circumstances. The crew got everyone safely off the plane and they waited for rescue teams to arrive."

"I'm guessing no one came."

Neville shrugged. "Maybe there were rescuers in the future, people who scoured the jungle for a plane that had vanished into thin air. But the place where they actually crashed, there was no one. No one even knew what had happened. Now, we can't know exactly when they arrived. The survivors kept the best records they could, but things were lost and forgotten. Our best estimate is that the plane crashed into this forest sometime around 1650."

Dorothy raised an eyebrow. "That's a very long time."

"Mm-hmm." He was now picking the last bits of meat from the melon rind. "Some of the survivors went in search of civilization. There are no records of what happened to them. Others remained at the crash site. They built shelters. There were supplies on the plane, but not much. Just enough to keep them alive, if not comfortable. They began to pair off, have babies. They sought out neighboring tribes for help with food. Within three generations, they had built their own little world in the ruins of the plane which had stranded them here."

"And now?"

"Skipping over a lot of history, now they are feared. They've spent the past three centuries absorbing their neighbors, killing the ones who refused to accept their dominance. Murder, pillage, destruction. They've built up their numbers and expanded to the point where they are now a threat to larger cities. Ketcham believes they're going to take over Belém within the next few weeks."

Dorothy said, "It's hard to imagine a threat of this magnitude going undetected."

"That's because they didn't exist before I arrived."

Dorothy laughed. "So all of this is a myth you've conjured?"

Neville shook his head. "If only it was that simple. I told you that this plane crossed through an unknown anomaly. That anomaly was created through my actions. When I discovered the Pratear, I set in motion a chain of events that would, five decades later, send a plane three hundred years into the past. History was immediately changed, but time isn't that fluid. Things have become unhinged here, at the epicenter of the event."

"Unhinged... how?"

"Like I said, there are two versions of me. I've seen him myself. I tried to kill him just to set things right, but... well... I don't know if you've ever been in a position to aim a gun at yourself, but it's incredibly hard to pull the trigger."

Dorothy said, "I suppose that makes sense."

"There are two paths," Neville said. "In one, the scourge of the Burnt Empire threatens to become unstoppable. In the other, there's still a chance to close the anomaly and prevent the plane from ever going back to the past."

"Meaning that all of this will cease to exist?" Dorothy asked.

"Presumably. Obviously I have no reference point to any of this. But it stands to reason that if we're successful, this branch of reality will never exist."

"A branch of reality which... I seem to be a part of."

He smiled sadly. "My apologies for that turn of events, Lady Boone, but I'll be signing my own death warrant as well. The only way to stop the children of the Burnt Empire from conquering the world is to ensure they never come to be in the first place."

Dorothy closed her eyes and took a deep breath.

"Untie me."

"I can't..."

"I'll help you," she said. "But I need to be untied to do it."

He stared at her, obviously uncertain as to whether he could believe her.

"I won't sacrifice my life for just anyone. Prove to me this Burnt Empire is as bad as you make them out to be, and I'll help you put an end to their carnage. No matter what the cost."

Neville considered for a long moment, then stood to undo her restraints.

CHAPTER NINE

THE NEXT time Trafalgar woke, she felt well enough to leave her bed. At some point, Cora - she hoped it had been Cora - had stripped her out of her mud- and blood-stained clothes and left her in a lightweight shift. Clean clothes were folded on the chair Cora had been using: a white cotton blouse and trousers. Trafalgar put them on, along with the boots which were standing next to the door, and ventured out.

It was still night, but the clearing outside her tent was ringed with lanterns that made it bright as day. There were more permanent shelters beyond the circle of light, and she saw shadowy forms of what she assumed to be watchmen moving between the trees. Felix was seated at the base of a torch, carving something from a piece of wood. When Trafalgar got close enough, she could see that it was a person. A woman, judging from the shape of it. When he held it up to examine his progress by the campfire's light, she realized she recognized its muse.

"She's unattached, as far as I know."

"Pardon?"

"Miss Hyde," Trafalgar said.

He smiled self-consciously and continued his work. "I assume you're feeling better?"

"Still not quite myself, but I believe I've spent far too much time lying down when there's work to be done. Cora explained to me what is required. I won't pretend to understand everything... your actions in the present affecting the future, which caused changes in the past..." She waved her hand.

"Perhaps because you see time as a strict forward progression of events. It may be easier to think of it as a web. Every decision we make has consequences. One morning you wake up and dash out the front door to begin your day. Or, alternatively, you decide to linger over breakfast and delay your departure by five minutes. Both situations are equally likely, so both paths exist in some form. We'll never know what happens in that other path, but I believe it is there, somewhere in the ether."

"A million billion threads based on every single person's every tiny decision?"

"Yes. And of course, sometimes threads intertwine. Maybe leaving early doesn't change anything. You arrive at work earlier in one timeline, but you run into a friend who delays you anyway. The two threads are once again united."

Trafalgar said, "Except in one I didn't have breakfast, so I would want a larger lunch."

Felix smiled. "Another thread."

"And you believe your arrival in the Amazon created a new thread, which somehow changed the past."

"I do. Did Cora tell you the legend?"

Trafalgar shook her head. "She had enough trouble trying to explain dual timelines to me."

Felix put down his knife. "Well, I suppose I've heard it enough times over the past year to give it a shot." He cleared his throat and leaned forward. "Many generations past, before the airships of the outside world rose above the clouds, the skies erupted. A great silver bird, gleaming like wet stone and lit from within by an unnatural flame, shattered through the firmament. It shook the ground when it landed, toppling trees. Fires spread for miles and the air was thick with a poisonous smell. The blood of the great bird seeped into the rivers, making it deadly to drink.

"The bird had riders. Gods who seemed human but spoke an unusual tongue and wore strange clothing. The local tribes helped these strangers, gave them food and provided shelter. The strangers were grateful at first. They learned how to communicate. They spoke of cooperation and living in harmony. But it soon became clear that their intentions were far from friendly."

Trafalgar had crouched during the story, and now she settled on the ground in a more comfortable position. "They began to dominate the local tribes, didn't they?"

"Well, once they had food and shelter, there was little reason to play nice. They set up in the ruins of a village their giant flying bird had destroyed. Soon the other tribes were warning each other to avoid the Burnt Empire. They were liars. They schemed to rule and destroy. They burned any villages who refused to swear fealty to them. Wars were fought. Countless lives lost."

Trafalgar said, "Astounding that none of this has been noticed by the outside world."

Felix said, "I'm certain it will be, once it has happened."

She stared at him. "I'm confused..."

"This village, the one providing refuge for us, is the one the Burnt Empire will crash into. Three hundred years ago. But as you can see, it is intact. The ripples haven't reached this spot yet. That's why the elders believe one version of history while the younger people remember something else."

"So you believe the legend is something that will actually occur?"

"The 'great silver bird' is an aeroplane, Miss Trafalgar. But not one that you or I would recognize. I believe it's a plane from the future. A plane that was sent back in time because of something I unleashed. I set the course of events in motion when I arrived here to find the Pratear. It was the first ripple in what will become a tidal wave. Fortunately, that wave has yet to reach our shores and wipe us out of existence."

Trafalgar shook her head. "This is madness."

"It's the truth as I've come to believe it. I discovered the Pratear and, in that act, created a situation which had ramifications I could never have imagined. It changed the people who live here. It changed their history. I have seen glimpses of the other reality. The one I created. There's another version of me there. We're both trying to make amends before this affects the rest of the world, but I believe if things are put right, one of us will have to die."

Trafalgar said, "It stands to reason that one timeline or another will eventually overtake the other, at which point you will... either cease to exist or combine with your double." A thought occurred to her. "There's also a chance that Dorothy survived in that version of events!"

"It's a possibility, yes."

"So by eliminating it, we will... we will effectively be killing her."

Felix shook his head. "She's already dead. This timeline is the true path. It is the result of how things played out before I interfered. We must set things right. Surely Lady Boone would agree as to what must be done."

Trafalgar grimaced rather than conceding his point. "So what do we have to do? You've had a year to fix things. Why haven't you?"

"It isn't quite as easy as flipping a switch and setting everything right. I've been thinking and rethinking my every move. Was the anomaly created due to what I did, or will it happen because of the actions I take to try setting it right? I've been learning how to communicate with the tribes in the area to learn use their wisdom, to plot a timeline of the changes. I cannot allow myself to make things worse."

"Meanwhile, your hesitation means the new timeline has come closer to replacing our own."

He ducked his head sheepishly. "There was already bleed-through from the moment I tried returning to the boat. My men were slaughtered by a tribe that hadn't existed twenty-four hours earlier. But you are correct. Waiting this long has allowed the two versions of reality to blur a bit at the edges. Even last month, Lady Boone would never have Slipped."

"Slipped?"

"Yes, Slipped or Slipping. That's what we call it when someone goes from..." He held his hand up and slid it to the side. "One to the other."

Trafalgar said, "So we can go there and save her."

"There's no guarantee you would be able to do that, or that you would be able to come back if you did. The only outcome where she survives is if she comes here. And like I said, there's no guarantee she could do that, if she's even alive there. It's best to assume we are on opposite sides of a river trying to ensure the flood takes out their shore instead of ours."

"I can't assume the worst yet. Not this early."

Felix said, "I sympathize. I felt the same way with the men from my expedition. I held out hope for as long as I could before I realized it was foolish to believe the Burnt Empire would take mercy on anyone they caught trespassing."

"They're truly that fierce?"

"They are... barbaric, and cunning. The native tribes, they're intelligent but they lack..." He searched for the right word. "They're naïve. They don't wage war the same way we do. The Empire took advantage of that. They took what we've learned from countless conflicts - along with whatever conflicts will occur between now and the era from which they hail - and applied it to people who are still fighting with spears and rudimentary weapons."

Trafalgar realized something. "If the Empire discovers we're trying to wipe them out..."

"That, my dear, is what has occupied the rest of my time here." He reached into the grass next to his hip and retrieved a revolver. He placed it on his thigh. "The Empire knows who I am and what I'm trying to do. They seem to know that if I'm successful, they'll cease to exist. They're doing everything in their power to stop me. The other Felix Neville has attempted to assassinate me on at least one occasion."

"My god."

"We have to stop them. I've been reluctant to enlist the villagers to assist me in another trek to the Pratear, but with you and Miss Hyde to offer assistance... there may be hope. If you're willing, of course."

"Absolutely," Trafalgar said.

He scanned the darkness behind her. "Your hopes that Lady Boone is alive on the other side has aroused a new concern in my mind."

"A concern?"

"Yes. I mentioned they were cunning. If your friend was alive after the ambush, they may have seen some value in taking her as a prisoner. They may be using her to ensure *they* survive."

Trafalgar shook her head. "Never. Dorothy would never help a group as terrible as this."

"She might if they lied to her. They could tell her that they're working against the Burnt Empire as well. If she believed she was working with the angels to stop a terrible tribe from taking over the world, she would join forces with them."

"Bloody hell," Trafalgar muttered. "You're right."

Felix rested his head against the torch and closed his eyes. "I was so relieved when you and Miss Hyde arrived. I thought at last I had gained the upper hand in this conflict. But it seems as if we've only kept the odds relatively even."

"It's worse than that, Captain Neville," Trafalgar said. "Dorothy Boone has been a friend of mine for several years but, before that, we were rivals. I've faced her as an adversary. And if she is indeed in this other timeline working against us, they most definitely have the upper hand."

He opened his eyes to stare at her. After a moment, he wiped a hand over his face and sighed heavily. "I hope you take this in the manner with which it's intended, Miss Trafalgar... but if that's the case, then I sincerely hope your friend died in the ambush."

Though she refused to say as much out loud, Trafalgar reluctantly agreed that it would be the best outcome for everyone.

The first thing Dorothy requested after being released from her restraints was a guide with a machete. She wanted to retrace their route back to the ambush site. They'd already lost so much time, but there was a chance she could find some trace of where Trafalgar and Cora had gone. Maybe they'd found refuge, maybe Eiriz or one of his men was still alive and would be waiting to take her to them. Neville refused.

"It's too close to nightfall. I'm sure you would prefer not to be wandering out in the wild considering what happened last time."

She bristled at his tone, but she couldn't deny he had a point. He suggested she instead spend her time exploring their camp. The village was more permanent than she expected. The huts had sturdy stone walls with sloping roofs made of thatched grasses. They were huddled together in a manner that allowed them to serve as a barrier against the rest of the forest. Ketcham, the man who had been there when she first regained consciousness, appointed himself as her unofficial guide.

"I assume this is the original settlement of the Burnt Empire."

"Repaired and rebuilt several times over the centuries," Ketcham said, "but for the most part, yes. This is where they lived when they first arrived from the past."

"Isn't it a bit reckless to set up camp here?"

He smiled. "It is a challenge. It is a statement that we aren't hiding from them. If they wish to attack us, they know where we can be found."

"As I said," Dorothy muttered. "Reckless."

Once they had gained some distance from the airplane, Dorothy turned to get a look at it from the outside. The shell was corroded and eaten away by rust, and most of the paint had chipped away to reveal the bare metal underneath.

"There's not a chance in hell this thing, whatever it might have once been, is three hundred years old. The metal wouldn't survive that long. The interiors..."

"A side effect of time being 'strange' here," Ketcham said. "Yes, this airplane arrived in the seventeenth century. But in a very real sense, it only came into existence a year ago. It's decaying at a very rapid rate. Trying to catch up with its new reality, I suppose. It's the most visible example we have of time trying to set itself right."

Dorothy muttered, "This is madness..." but she couldn't deny the evidence of her own eyes.

Neville approached with a plate of beans and a large chunk of what smelled like fresh cornbread. Dorothy's stomach twisted so violently with hunger that she was almost afraid she wouldn't be able to eat anything even if it was offered. She swallowed to ensure she wouldn't drool when she spoke.

"Where did you get~?"

"This is for you." He handed her the plate. Dorothy's fingers tightened on the edge of it, almost trembling from the effort of not digging in. "I thought you might be a bit ravenous following everything you've been through. There's more where that came from if you're still hungry when you're finished."

She said, "Thank you," and took a bite of the bread as casually as she could. It melted on her tongue, rich and hot and buttery. She had taken three more bites before she realized, and she forced herself to chew and swallow before taking another. "My... compliments to the chef," she said once her mouth was free again.

Neville smiled. "You're certainly welcome. I suggest you spend the rest of the night satisfying your hunger and getting a proper rest. In the morning, we'll set out."

"Set out? Where are we going?"

"The Pratear, Lady Boone."

She raised an eyebrow. "So quickly?"

"Time is fluid, but it's moving like a river. We don't know how long it will be until the two paths merge. The sooner we're underway, the sooner this whole mess can be remedied once and for all. So enjoy your meal. Tomorrow will be a very busy day."

Dorothy watched him go. Ketcham was still with her, but Dorothy didn't care what he thought about her manners. She shoved the rest of the cornbread into her mouth, still chewing it as she went in search of a second helping.

CHAPTER TEN

Felix scheduled their departure for dawn, and Trafalgar went back to her tent to get as much sleep as she could. In the morning she woke to the sound of the team preparing to set out. She dressed and wrapped a scarf around her head, tucking its excess length into the collar of her blouse. Cora poked her head in and smiled when she saw Trafalgar was almost ready to leave.

"I was skeptical when Captain Neville said you would be joining us, but you certainly look as if you've made a miraculous recovery. How do you feel?"

"I believe I'm well enough to make the journey. But I'm grateful you will be there with us, just in case. I'm not entirely certain I trust Neville yet."

Cora glanced over her shoulder and moved deeper into the tent. "You think he's lying?"

"Not necessarily. But his comment about Dorothy being misled by his... 'other' made me think we could be in a similar situation. He told us his side of the story and claims his cause is just, and we believe him because he's the one we happened to meet. He claims the Burnt Empire are savages who must be stopped. We have no way of knowing how biased he might be. We should take any facts he presents to us with a grain of salt."

"I concur. I've spent the morning wandering as much as the villagers will allow me. I was trying to find one of these 'Slipping' points he was talking about."

"Trying to leave me behind and join Dorothy on her side?"

Cora grinned. "Well, I assume she would be much less hassle. But no, I was merely trying to confirm they were as difficult to find as he claimed. All I can say for certain is that I didn't happen to find any during my brief search."

"I'm glad to see you're maintaining skepticism, despite..."

"Despite what?" Cora said.

Trafalgar smiled. "Oh, please. I may have been feverish the past day or so, but it seems clear the two of you have built a rapport. I can't fault you for it. A dashing explorer, lost in the jungle. It's all very romantic. I'm sure it's helped by the fact that he's been all on his own for a year, and you've kept yourself cooped up in your house since leaving the institute. It's only natural for the two of you to gravitate toward one another. Just keep your head clear."

Cora said, "Of course." She folded her arms over her chest and smiled. "He is dashing, isn't he?"

Trafalgar laughed and ushered Cora out of her tent.

Felix was standing with a group of villagers, the first Trafalgar had seen since her arrival. They looked at her with a combination of fear and curiosity, and she nodded to them in what she hoped was a universal greeting. One of them was holding a leather bag which another was filling with tightly-wrapped packages.

"Miss Trafalgar, meet a few of our hosts. This is Matta and his brother, Viejas. They've offered to accompany us on our journey to the Pratear."

"Wonderful," Trafalgar said. "It's wonderful to meet you, gentlemen."

She offered her hand, but they only stared at it. Matta, the one holding the bag, muttered something so quietly that she couldn't even tell what language it was.

"They're a bit shy with new people," Felix said. "Especially women. This morning was the first time any of them even looked Miss Hyde in the eye."

"I think the time has come for you to call me Cora, Felix," she said.

He smiled and looked away. "Perhaps I will."

Trafalgar pretended to ignore the flirtation. She turned to scan the area, which was now only slightly more visible than it had been at night. The canopy overhead created a near-solid barrier that prevented sunlight from reaching them.

"How long do you think this trek will be?"

"I've been back and forth to the site a few times since the original incident. We should arrive by nightfall, barring any unexpected delays. We'll camp there while you and M... you and *Cora* investigate the anomaly. If we can come to an agreement on the proper course of action, we'll finally put an end to this situation."

Trafalgar said, "If we succeed in closing or preventing the anomaly, how long will it be before we see results?"

"The changes were apparent immediately, so I assume the reverse would be true. No anomaly means no plane crash, no Burnt Empire, and no alternate timeline. It will be like the sun breaking through clouds after a storm." He took the bag from Matta and slipped his arms through the straps. Trafalgar saw a second bag containing their camping gear and took it for herself before one of the men could insist on taking it. Felix watched her put it on but said nothing. "Well, ladies, if we're ready?"

"Lead the way, Captain," Trafalgar said.

Dorothy spent the rest of the night in the wreckage of the plane. It seemed better than staying in one of the cabins and trusting Neville's men. They seemed afraid of the plane and gave it a wide berth, so that was where she wanted to be. She woke to find it did seem as if a few years had passed in terms of decay. The metal was more corroded, and the structure creaked when she climbed out of the gaping hole in the back. Neville was nowhere to be found, but someone was crouching next to the table where all the food had been laid out the night before. There were four bags sitting on the ground next to the table, all of them standing open like baby birds awaiting a meal from their mother. The person, tall and strapping, with sleeves cut off to reveal arms roped with muscles, was loading supplies into the bags.

Dorothy cleared her throat as she approached. "I don't suppose there are any leftovers."

"Anything that wasn't packed away last night is going in the supplies for the people going to the Pratear. Are you one of them?"

"You're a woman!" Dorothy was unable to stop herself from blurting it out. She blinked and shook her head. "I'm sorry, I didn't know there were any women in the group."

She ignored the reaction. Her short hair, combined with the lean build, probably meant she had dealt with the confusion more often than she'd like. Instead, she continued her work with barely a glance back at Dorothy.

"You're that woman they brought in the other day. The new one."

"Yes, that's right. Dorothy Boone. And yes, I am one of the people accompanying Captain Neville on the trip to Pratear."

The woman looked her up and down. "You don't look like much."

"I'm more formidable than I appear. I've made it this far, haven't I?"

"A little worse for wear." She tapped her brow above the forehead.

Dorothy frowned and reached up. There was a bandage just below her hairline. She hadn't even noticed it the day before when she was speaking to Neville and Ketcham.

"I've had worse," she said, trying to cover her surprise. "And you have me at a disadvantage. You didn't tell me your name."

"Rute."

"A... beautiful name."

The woman grunted and lifted the bag she'd been filling with food. "It's going to take all day to reach the river. It won't be easy. I'm not just talking about the terrain. On a nuisance level, there are insects. They bite and irritate your skin. They get in your nose and mouth and eyes. There will be snakes and spiders."

"Lions and tigers and bears, oh my," Dorothy sang.

Rute glared at her. "There will also be people. Savages."

"I don't believe there's such a thing as 'savages,' to be honest. People who are less advanced than us, of course, but to imply they're less human simply because--"

"This isn't a scholarly discussion, Lady Boone. This isn't some debate you're having in the sitting room after dinner. Call them what you like, but we're invading their territory. They react as savagely as you or I would if someone broke into our homes. They will be attacking us with arrows, with spears and bone knives, and they will not speak our language. You will not be able to reason with them. So forgive me for employing a shorthand to warn you about the people who will be trying to kill you in a few hours."

"Message received."

Ketcham had approached without her hearing him, but he'd apparently overheard some of their exchange. "Don't let Rute scare you, Lady Boone. She's just feeling a little intimidated having another girl in the camp for a change."

Rute snorted and went back to packing the food.

"Where's Captain Neville?"

"Still asleep," Ketcham said. "He trusts us to get everything ready, and he'll join us when we set out. He gets headaches in the morning. Dizzy spells. It usually happens when the 'other' Felix Neville is awake first. It throws him for a loop."

Dorothy said, "I can imagine. So... you believe this whole scenario is true? That there's another timeline with a second version of the captain?"

"We've seen evidence of it," Rute said. "We went out hunting a few months ago. Came back here, and the entire clearing was gone. No plane. Nothing, no sign any of us had ever been here. We thought we had the wrong place. Wandered for a bit. Took about three days before it snapped back to the right version."

"It's hard to believe that anything we do now can prevent something that happened three centuries ago."

"Then don't think about it that way," Ketcham said. "Think of it as an ongoing event which began a year ago and will continue for five decades. The dam is leaking and we have a chance to prevent a flood even as we're drowning in it."

"That does help. Thank you, Mr. Ketcham." She moved closer to the packs. "Is there anything I can do to speed along the process?"

Rute hesitated, then gave Dorothy a list of tasks to complete. As Dorothy went about them, she let her mind wander to Trafalgar and Cora. She had to believe they were still alive, even if they might be hurt. She also had to believe they were in the 'other' timeline, the 'proper' events, so that they were spared when the anomaly was closed. She wondered if they knew where she was. If they'd fled the ambush while she was still unconscious, they might have been forced to write her off as dead. That would be the best possibility. It meant they would be able to leave the forest, get back to their lives in London...

She rested her hand on top of a pack. London. Beatrice, waiting at home for her. Her throat closed up at the thought of never seeing Trix again. She would never know for certain what had happened.

"Boone?"

She turned and saw Neville had woken. His hair was wet and pushed back out of his face, but his beard was tangled. Though he was dressed, he looked as if he'd only woken up thirty seconds before saying her name. Ketcham and Rute were standing behind him, already wearing their packs.

"Is everything all right?"

"Perfectly fine." She cinched the bag and slung it over her shoulder. "Are we ready to depart?"

Neville looked up at the canopy. "Sun's rising, so there will be more light once we're underway. Try to keep up, Lady Boone."

He brushed past Ketcham and headed for the trees. Dorothy adjusted the strap of her pack and brought up the rear behind Rute.

CHAPTER ELEVEN

THE SUN may have been unable to break through the canopy, but the heat of the day quickly made its presence known. Dorothy was swarmed by tiny black bugs she could barely see, let alone identify. She protected her eyes by wearing a pair of sunglasses loaned to her by Ketcham and did her best to swat away anything that got too close to her nose or mouth.

"I know your reputation, Lady Boone," Neville called back. "You've traveled the world." He grunted as he chopped through a thick vine. "But you haven't spent much time in jungles, have you?"

"Not if I can avoid it," Dorothy said. "I'm not against living rough when it's absolutely necessary, but I also believe there are places in the world that are simply not worth the trouble."

"There are mysteries to be unearthed in every corner of the globe, Dorothy," Neville said. "Your comfort is a small price to pay for the advancement of knowledge!"

Dorothy nodded. "That is true. But I believe secrets reveal themselves when they are ready to be known. Perhaps this is nature's way of preventing anyone from finding the Pratear and causing the calamity we're now trying to prevent."

"A time for everything, and everything in its time," Neville said. "Sounds like an excuse to be lazy."

"Lazy, never!" Dorothy huffed. "There's more than enough waiting to be found all over the world. We'll get to it all in due time. I just think it's wiser to start with the things right in front of us."

Neville said, "Well, to each their own. Plenty of treasures for everyone to find. I'm content to let you bounce around to the more accessible sites while I take my time to dig out the truly impressive discoveries."

Dorothy sighed and shook her head.

Ketcham looked back and smiled. He was close enough to Dorothy to speak in a low voice that didn't carry to Neville. "You don't have to like someone in order to work with them."

"Lucky for him," she said. "Less so for us."

Neville had ascended a small rise, his boots more or less at eye level for the rest of them, and held up a hand to indicate they should stop. He turned and pointed at Ketcham, waving for him to come up. Rute assumed a firing position, her feet planted in the spongy grass. Neville and Ketcham moved to take cover behind trees, leaving a space between them. Dorothy wasn't entirely certain what was expected of her, since she hadn't been offered a weapon, so she crouched to make herself less of a target to any threat that might present itself.

Ketcham whispered a question. "...here or the other side?"

Neville shook his head. "Can't tell."

Dorothy moved closer. Rute hissed at her, but Dorothy ignored the warning as she joined the men at the hill's peak. Neville looked at her with an irritated scowl, but he didn't risk verbally scolding her. Directly ahead of them, she saw a weak stream trickling across a stony bed. It was closer to a series of miniature waterfalls than a river. A line of men were using the stones as a walkway to follow the ground's gentle ascent. They were all naked from the waist up and their dark skin was covered with painted markings. They wore trousers and belts but no shoes. Several of them were carrying corpses of small animals bundled together on sticks.

"Children of the Burnt Empire coming back from a hunt," Ketcham whispered. "Descendants of the people who arrived on the airplane. Future generations of people who most likely haven't even been born yet."

"I assume there was some amount of interbreeding with the local tribes."

Neville said, "That's normally how it works. A combination of the best genes from both parties. The natives knew how to survive in the forest and the plane passengers were savvy in other ways. It's part of what makes them so formidable."

"Their camp must be near here," Ketcham said. "We could follow them. Forget about changing the past and just stop them here, in the present."

Dorothy said, "You're talking about genocide."

Ketcham shrugged. "I'm suggesting the slaughter of people who shouldn't exist in the first place. If we succeed in closing the anomaly, they'll never be born. What's the difference?"

"The amount of blood on our hands," Dorothy said.

Neville shook his head. "Ketcham is correct. The end result would be the same."

"Not for the people who were killed when the plane crashed. Not for the tribes that have been wiped out by the Burnt Empire in the centuries since they arrived."

"The loss of those primitives will hardly affect the rest of the world," Neville grumbled.

Dorothy grimaced. "A lovely point of view. We simply have no way of knowing how the world was affected the anomaly. By the loss of life, by the countless tribes being wiped out. There could be consequences we won't be aware of for years or decades, if they're even obvious in our lifetimes. The plane crash should never have happened. The only solution is to close the anomaly and erase this timeline."

Ketcham checked his weapon and pushed himself up. "I have a better idea. We kill these bastards, and then we let time do what it wants. We can preserve this timeline and we all get to live. I don't care about some damn tribesmen. I care about *myself*, and I'm going to do what needs to be done."

He was on his feet by the end of his speech. He had only taken a single step when a branch hit him from behind. He crumpled like tissue paper and dropped his gun, his spot on the hill taken by Rute. She tossed away the branch and bent down to pick up Ketcham's weapon, turning it so she could extend it to Dorothy butt-first.

"You're right," she said. "We won't fix this by blunt force. We have to set things right. Captain Neville, you just spoke of the worth of doing things the hard way. What you're talking about doing... killing these men and letting everything else stay wrong... that is the lazy path."

Neville stared at her, and then looked toward the men. All but the last pair had disappeared through the trees. He watched until they were gone, then pushed himself up. He brushed the leaves and dirt from his clothes and sighed as he moved back down the hill.

"Wake him up. I'm not dragging his dead weight all the way to the river."

"Stop, stop..." Felix dropped down and waved the rest of their group to do the same.

Trafalgar was grateful for the chance to catch her breath. Cora also looked relieved as she leaned her shoulder against a tree. Felix was tireless, marching into the forest as if he didn't have to worry about pacing himself. She had first checked to make sure there were no ants or spiders camouflaged by the bark before she risked touching it. They were both dripping with sweat and panting, though Felix looked as fresh as a man out for a morning stroll. Matta and Viejas, bringing up the rear, also dropped down. They looked more weary than Cora. Trafalgar had a canteen of water hanging from her belt and uncapped it, offering it to Matta. He hesitated, then took it with a nod of gratitude.

Ahead, in the clearing, Trafalgar saw what had made Felix stop: a line of men were moving through the jungle in a slow but steady march. The leader was tall but slouched, his head swinging back and forth as if his neck couldn't keep it still. The blade of his machete was darkened either by rust or dried blood. She counted seven of them already in the clearing but there were still more coming out of the underbrush. Several of them were carrying animal corpses still bloody from killing blows.

"Slippage," Felix said. "This is part of the other timeline."

"How can you tell?"

He held out his hand, closed one eye, and lined his fingers up with a nearby tree. "There's a shimmer in the air. It takes some effort to notice it but, once you do, it's hard to miss."

"So this is a thin space? Theoretically, we could pass through to the other side and find Dorothy."

Felix sighed. "Theoretically. Even if you found her, I doubt she would appreciate you jumping off a cliff just to die with her." He twisted to look back at her. "I say this with as much compassion as I can muster, Miss Trafalgar. You have to consider Lady Boone a casualty of this mission. Otherwise we will all be lost, and the world as we know it is doomed."

Trafalgar pressed her lips together and watched the marching men. "These are members of that tribe you mentioned, yes? Descendants of the people who arrived here from the future?"

"I believe so, yes."

It was difficult for her to wrap her mind around the fact she was looking at people who shouldn't exist, who would in fact never be born if they were successful. She recalled what Felix had said about them. She knew they were brutal, they'd slaughtered and destroyed anyone who stood in their way, but there were plenty of so-called 'good' armies that had done the same thing. Hell, the British Empire couldn't claim it was any better than these men.

"Perhaps we should follow them," she said. "We can talk to them on their own ground..."

Felix stared at her as if she was crazed. "They would slit your throat before you could get a single word out. These are not men who can be reasoned with. There is no strategy you can suggest which would make them decide to wipe themselves from the pages of history. As far as I can tell, they've never figured out the Pratear is the source of the anomaly. If they knew that, they would defend it with to their dying breath. Any interaction with them would be futile at best, self-destructive at worst."

Trafalgar said, "It was merely a suggestion."

"A poor one," Felix muttered.

Cora offered a look of commiseration. "I don't think it hurts to at least raise the possibility. But I do agree with Felix. The less we have to interact with these people, the better."

Trafalgar nodded. The men were almost out of the clearing now. She knew how easily looks could deceive, how even the worst men could look normal in the proper setting, but these looked like simple men who were providing for their families. They were out hunting early in the morning. They were exhausted. They were just *men*, for god's sake, when Felix had been selling her monsters. She wanted a better narrative. She wanted another side of the story before she declared an entire tribe worthy of extinction.

Once the last man had vanished, Felix stood and stretched his legs. "Do you ladies need to rest a while longer, or shall we resume our journey?"

Trafalgar would have liked another few minutes, if she was being entirely honest, but she knew Felix would take that as a mark of weakness. Viejas handed back her canteen, which she noticed the two of them had nearly drained. She took a drink for herself, glanced at Cora to make sure she was ready to continue, then stood and adjusted her scarf.

"Lead the way, Captain."

CHAPTER TWELVE

THEY STOPPED for lunch earlier than Dorothy expected. Neville used Ketcham's condition as an excuse, and she had to admit the man did look quite shell-shocked. Rute apparently hadn't gone easy on him when she clubbed his skull. But despite the plausibility of his reasoning, she believed the trip was far more taxing on the captain than he wanted to admit. He was the first to drop onto a stone, mopping his face and neck with a rag that looked positively soaked when he returned it to his pack. His face was red and he struggled to catch his breath even after everyone else seemed settled.

Whatever the cause of their respite, Dorothy was grateful for the chance to sit and appreciate the beauty of the world in which they found themselves. Creatures chittered high above them in the trees, and she watched as a couple leapt from one branch to another. It was almost as if they were actually flying, though she could have sworn they were squirrels. Or maybe bats...

"Something has been bothering me," she said, hoping to sound casual. "Maybe you could enlighten me, Captain."

He gestured for her to continue.

"It's going to take us most of the day to reach the Pratear from the airplane. Presumably, it will take us another day to make the trek back. According to Eiriz, you and your men were in the jungle for three days before he went looking and found the slaughter."

"That sounds correct."

"It doesn't leave much time for exploring. You must have known precisely where you were going when you arrived in Belém."

He smiled. "Come now, Dorothy. Certainly you know that a great deal of exploration happens at home, in dusty libraries and hunched over old maps."

Dorothy nodded. "Yes, of course. But to find something as evasive as the Pratear, you must have had a very good source. Even the people who live here wrote it off as a myth long ago. How did you know where to find it?"

Neville closed his eyes. It took him so long to begin speaking that Dorothy almost thought he'd fallen asleep, but his voice was steady and strong.

"A message. The last time I was in Brazil, a message was delivered to me. It said the Pratear was real, it gave the coordinates, and told me that I would find riches beyond my wildest dreams. Of course, at that point, I had run out of funds so I had to return to London. I had to convince the RGS to finance another expedition. I suppose in a way, the mission was a success."

Dorothy said, "You've lost everything. Your team was decimated. It's highly unlikely you'll receive funding for another expedition once we return to London and tell the tale of what happened."

"A Pyrrhic victory, to be sure, but a victory nonetheless." He opened his canteen and lifted it to take a drink, but found it empty. "Damn."

Dorothy passed him hers, and he nodded his thanks.

"Someone wanted you to find the river," she surmised.

Neville shrugged. "It's possible."

It was a mystery Dorothy didn't want or need to deal with. She had a feeling simply closing the anomaly would be enough of a task without worrying about a conspiracy.

"As long as we're stopped here," she said, "perhaps you can tell us more about how you opened the anomaly. What happened when you found the river?"

Again, Neville took nearly a minute before he answered. "Deceptive. The name, it's deceptive. People look for a river, they look for a ribbon of water curling through the trees. But from the surface, the only visible part of the river looks like a lake. When I first reached the coordinates, I thought I'd been hoodwinked. But I refused to give up. I could feel something special about the place.

"One of my men was actually the one who found it. A crack in the world, mostly covered by the undergrowth. It was just a few meters wide, so of course we were drenched by passing though it to the other side. We found ourselves in a cave which seemed to have been carved by the river. It sloped downward into the Earth. Our lights didn't reach the bottom, but we could hear the water splashing. We knew it had to be a relatively short drop. We found handholds in the stone, so we ventured deeper."

Dorothy said, "How far down was it?"

"I don't know."

She furrowed her brow. "I don't need an exact measurement, but a general idea of how deep the cave is would help."

"I don't recall anything after we decided to make the descent." He showed his palms and shrugged. "As I've told you, I've been back to the site to try fixing this problem myself. The one thing I didn't mention is that I have started to fear I'm part of the problem. That whatever erased my memory of that first visit also prevents me from seeing the solution. That is why I'm so hopeful for your presence, Lady Boone. It is my sincere hope that your fresh eyes can finally provide the missing pieces of the puzzle."

Dorothy glared at him. "I don't appreciate being kept in the dark like this, Captain Neville. I still would have come with you even if you'd shared this back at the airplane."

"Nothing has changed. The goal remains the same. We must find a way to set things right."

Rute surprised them all by speaking up. "If you don't remember what happened underground, how can you be sure you were the one who caused the anomaly?"

Neville said, "Who else could it have been?"

Dorothy realized what the other woman was implying. "The note had to come from somewhere. You recruited me as a set of fresh eyes. Maybe someone did the same thing with you."

"I supposed that's a possibility."

"Whoever it was may have known the anomaly was bad, but it hadn't grown large enough to have visible consequences. By the time you arrived, it was large enough to create two timelines. Who knows how powerful it will be when we reach it now."

Rute stood up. "All the more reason to stop sitting around chattering. Let's get a move on."

Dorothy was willing, and even the silent and concussed Ketcham didn't argue, but Neville took longer than any of them to get his pack on.

"Are you certain you're up to the rest of this journey?" Dorothy asked. "Perhaps you should give us the coordinates and go back to camp. You look absolutely wrecked."

"We're halfway there. It will take as much effort to continue onward as it would to go back." He took a deep breath and blew it out hard. "Come along, Lady Boone."

She watched him follow Rute and brought up the rear so she could keep an eye on both Neville and Ketcham to make sure neither of them collapsed on the path.

They made excellent time to their destination, owing to the breakneck pace Felix set. Trafalgar felt as if they'd been running a marathon by the time he finally lifted a hand to indicate they could stop. Cora's hair had come loose from the braid she'd put it in that morning and tumbled across her shoulder like a dead creature. Matta and Viejas were faring better, most likely accustomed to running over this terrain, but she could see gratefulness in their eyes as well.

Felix extended his arms wide and turned to face them with a beatific smile. "This is it."

"This is the river?" Trafalgar said. She scanned the clearing but could only see what appeared to be a large lake.

Felix said, "This is the endpoint of the river. So easy to overlook the truth beneath the surface." He moved closer and pointed. "There. Do you see? The rise in the ground, that outcropping of stone? It seems to create a cove but if you look closer..."

Cora had moved closer. "It continues underground."

"Indeed it does! This is where all of our troubles began." He continued forward.

"You still haven't explained exactly how the troubles began," Trafalgar pointed out, "or how you intend to correct it."

Felix didn't slow his pace or look back. "It's too complicated to explain before you know everything. Once we're in the cave, you'll see for yourself."

Trafalgar stopped walking. Cora, uncertain, also stopped at her side. Felix realized they were falling behind and finally faced them again.

"What's wrong?"

"You don't know how to fix this. All your vagueness, the lack of a solid plan, your repeated trips back here over the course of the year." She looked at Matta and Viejas. "Has he ever explained to you or anyone in the tribe exactly what happened? Or told you what needs to be set right?"

Felix said, "There's no way they would understand. They're savages!"

"This is their *home*," Cora snapped. "They likely understand it better than you ever could."

The two tribesmen looked uncomfortable at being caught in the middle of the argument. Viejas was the one who finally spoke. "He says too dangerous for us to worry. Says we only get in way."

"We can speak in your language if it's easier," Cora said, then switched to Portuguese. "Do you know anything about what happened a year ago?"

Matta also switched to Portuguese. "This is not our language, either. But we speak it better than yours." He pointed at Felix. "He only told us something bad happened at the river. He told us to keep our distance, that it was his problem to fix. At first we tried to convince him we knew the forest better than any Englishman, but then... then things began to change. The 'Slipping' he talks about, the changes in our elders' memories. We started to believe that maybe he was correct. We didn't know what was happening, but we knew our home wasn't the same as it used to be."

Cora paraphrased what he'd said for Trafalgar, who turned on Felix. "You can't claim we're too ignorant to understand. So please, enlighten us. How exactly did this fiasco begin and what, exactly, do you need from us to set things right?"

Felix hung his head, shoulders sagging. "Damn... I don't know, all right? I don't bloody know. I don't even remember what happened when I was in the cave. My men and I descended, and the next thing I can recall is making my way through the forest back to the river. I knew we'd spent time underground, doing something, and I knew my mission was finished. But details escaped me. And it was already clear that things were different."

"Damn it," Trafalgar said. "So we have no idea what's actually waiting for us down below. It could literally be anything!"

"Whatever it is," Cora said, "we can assume it isn't physically dangerous. Felix and his men were able to leave without injury. Were any of your men bloody or hurt when they returned to the surface?"

Felix said, "Not until we encountered the Burnt Empire tribesmen."

"That should be some comfort," Cora said. "Minor. Fleeting. But comfort nonetheless."

Trafalgar sighed and shook her head. "We've come too far to retreat now. But Felix remains in the lead position. If there is someone hostile down there, they might recognize him and be more amenable to his return."

"I believe that would be more than fair," Felix said. "Shall we?"

"No sense in stopping now."

Trafalgar noticed a change in the air as they approached the lake. It was a subtle shift in the air, something she wouldn't have noticed if she wasn't paying extremely close attention to her surroundings. Felix approached the overgrowth that hid the underground entrance and used his machete to cut away the extra foliage. Water cascaded over a stone lip, into a dark gap, and she could hear the echo of its splash far below. He started to speak, but stopped and choked on the unspoken words.

"Captain?" Trafalgar moved closer. "Is everything all right?"

"Fine, I... I think..." He looked at her and Cora as if he'd never seen them before. His face shifted and, for a moment, his skin was filthy with sweat. Even stranger, his beard was gone and then back in the space of a blink. Before she could say anything, his eyes widened and he brought up a pistol she could have sworn he hadn't been carrying before. "Rute! Look out!"

She turned and saw a man rushing at her with a club raised above his head, mouth opened in a scream she couldn't hear. She planted her feet on the muddy ground, dropped her shoulder, and grabbed the man's arm as soon as it was close enough. She used his momentum against him, rolling him across her shoulders and hurling him into the water. Felix cried out in pain, but she didn't have time to deal with him. Another attacker, barefoot and bare-chested like the first but clad in trousers, had knocked Cora to the ground. Trafalgar drew her gun and shot him in the chest before he could further his attack.

The gun was knocked from her hand by a club she hadn't seen until just before it made contact. She swore under her breath as the latest attacker wrapped his arms around her waist and shoved her backward. Her foot slipped in the mud and she toppled into the water. The man she had tossed in earlier grabbed hold of her shirt and gave a primal yell as he threw her toward the cave entrance. Water rushed all around her, pushing her closer to the edge. She had no idea how far the fall was or how deep the water at the bottom might be, but it seemed as if she was about to find out in the worst possible~

She was grabbed by the collar, her momentum stalled long enough for an arm to slip under hers.

"Good lord, but you're heavy!"

The voice was unexpected but gloriously familiar. Trafalgar held on tightly and pushed her feet against the mud and stone to assist in her own salvation. They reached the shore and Trafalgar was released onto the grass. She pushed herself up on her hands, coughed up the water she had swallowed, and twisted to confirm what she'd heard was true.

Dorothy Boone, soaked to the skin, gasping for breath and rubbing her shoulder. Dorothy looked at her with relief in her eyes which matched that which Trafalgar felt. Trafalgar stood and stared at the other woman as if she was a mirage which could disappear at any moment.

"I'm not saying I regret doing it," Dorothy said, "but honestly, how much do you weigh?"

"You're alive," Trafalgar said.

Dorothy smiled. "As are you. We may be a little worse for wear, but I think~"

Trafalgar grabbed Dorothy's face and kissed her. The kiss was too brief and Dorothy's shock too overpowering for her to respond before it ended.

"That was unexpected," Dorothy said, her voice softer than Trafalgar had ever heard.

"I apologize." Trafalgar blinked away the moisture in her eyes, hoping Dorothy dismissed it as lake water. "I hadn't realize how thoroughly I had given up hope of ever seeing you again."

Dorothy awkwardly plucked at her wet clothes. "Well, I suppose... I hadn't stopped long enough to consider the same. But I'm grateful to see you appear to be in one piece. And Cora..." She turned to gesture and saw Cora grappling with one of the shirtless men. "Oh, crumbs!"

Trafalgar ran to Cora's aide, but another woman got there first. She grabbed the native by his long hair, pulled him back, and grabbed his throat in a crushing grip. She dropped him and spun on the ball of her foot to attack one of the other natives.

"Rute, Trafalgar," Dorothy said. "Trafalgar, this is Rute. She is a frightening woman, but I've found it helpful to be on her good side, and she's proven to be the most reasonable member of the group."

"Noted."

Rute grunted.

Matta and Viejas were also fighting, their faces and shirts bloodied but apparently winning their respective bouts. Trafalgar looked to see Felix was slumped where she had last seen him, twitching but seemingly unconscious. Cora got off two shots and dropped one of the natives. This was apparently enough to convince the attackers that the tide had turned against them. Those who were still on their feet switched to defensive tactics so those on the ground could get up and flee.

"Looks as if we've won," Dorothy said once all the men had vanished into rustling brush.

"So it would seem," Trafalgar agreed. "We're fortunate you came along when you did. Where *did* you come from, anyway?"

Dorothy said, "Those men, residents of the Burnt Empire, attacked us not far from here. We tried to fight them off, but Captain Neville insisted we continue on. He thought if we could reach the cave, they would stop following us. Some superstition. We arrived here and it was as though we were walking through a fog. You all looked like ghosts to us."

Trafalgar said, "I, for one, am grateful you recognized us when you did." She looked at Matta and Viejas, who were now tending to Cora's injuries. The woman Dorothy called Rute was kneeling next to a man Trafalgar had thought was with their attackers. "I assume that either you Slipped into our timeline or we Slipped into yours."

"You know about the Slipping theory?"

"Mm. Captain Neville explained it to us. Did you have someone from his expedition in your timeline to explain it to you?"

Dorothy looked at Felix. He was still unconscious in the grass. "Yes. Captain Neville. He also said there were two versions of him in the forest, but if he was with you..."

Trafalgar walked over to the captain and rolled him over. He had a wild, unkempt beard and looked like he had been dragged across rocky terrain to his current position. "The man I spent the past few days with was clean-shaven and spent the past day moving like an Olympian. I assume this is the one from your timeline."

"You're wrong." Everyone looked at Cora. "This is their version of Captain Neville, but it's also ours. The timelines merged. That's why we're all here together."

Dorothy said, "That... Is that..."

"I don't know if it means we're too late to stop history from changing," Cora said. "It may simply be a side effect of our proximity to the source. But if I were a betting woman, I would say we should make haste while we still have a chance to stop this madness."

CHAPTER THIRTEEN

"I THINK we should discuss the kiss."

Trafalgar grunted. "Do you believe... our current situation is the optimal time for that conversation?"

"Well," Dorothy craned her neck to search for the next handhold. She found it, moved her hand, then risked moving her foot from the narrow ledge on which it rested. "We're both the type to simply ignore something like that. We find ourselves in a moment of relative calm, when we might as well be talking, and I think that is the most pressing topic we could cover."

Tiny pebbles rained down on her. She squeezed her eyes shut until the small rockslide ended, then glanced up. Trafalgar was approximately half a meter above her on the stone wall. They were close to the halfway point of the cliff, which she estimated to be approximately ten meters high. Sunlight and water streamed through the cave entrance above them. They were close enough to the waterfall that Dorothy could feel its spray on her cheeks, but she and Trafalgar were both already so thoroughly soaked that it barely registered.

"You kissed me."

"Yes, I'm well aware." Trafalgar took a deep breath. "I had been told you were most likely dead. I didn't want to believe it, but the majority of the evidence did imply that conclusion. So while I tried to hold out hope, a larger part of me accepted the fact you were gone. And then there you were, saving my life, like some sort of dazzling angel. I was overwhelmed with emotion."

Dorothy moved down another step. She could see the cave floor below her, a jagged ledge between the river and the wall.

"So there's no need for a discussion?"

"Beyond the one we're having now? No, I don't believe so."

Dorothy said, "No lingering feelings?"

"None that I'm aware of."

"Was that... blast!"

Trafalgar's boots scraped on the stone. "Are you all right?"

"Yes, I just grabbed a particularly sharp rock. I was going to ask if that was your first experience kissing another woman."

"Ah. It was. And to answer the question you're actually asking, I had never considered being with a woman romantically or sexually before we made our acquaintance. Seeing you and Beatrice together made me consider the possibilities of a Sapphic relationship. I don't know if I would ever take the leap. I am still very attracted to men. But perhaps if I met someone, I would be open to all options. Does that answer your question?"

"It does, thank you. I'm just glad to know kissing me didn't sour you on the idea of kissing women."

"Hardly." There was laughter in her voice. "In fact, when we return to London, I intend to tell Beatrice she is a very fortunate woman."

"I'm the fortunate one," Dorothy said softly. Her foot touched a wide, flat surface and she looked to confirm she had reached the bottom. She stepped away from the wall and rolled her shoulders, then examined her fingers to gauge the severity of any cuts or scrapes she had endured from the climb. A half dozen red marks of various length covered the pads. "Hm. I should have worn gloves."

"You weren't wearing gloves?"

Dorothy rolled her eyes, then turned to examine where she was as she waited for Trafalgar to join her. It was a tall tower of stone, with the Pratear River accumulating in a shallow pool before continuing on through a diamond-shaped hole in the far wall. Neville and Ketcham obviously hadn't been in any state to make the descent, so Cora volunteered to stay on solid ground to watch over them. Rute, along with Trafalgar and Cora's compatriots, were acting as security to ensure the Burnt Empire didn't attack again.

Trafalgar reached the bottom and brushed the dirt from her clothes as she caught her breath. "I have to say, I do enjoy this aspect of our partnership."

"The incredibly dangerous part, where we're potentially trapped in a dark underground tomb with who knows what ahead of us?"

Trafalgar smiled. "Yes, actually. When it's just the two of us against who-knows-what. I had a sense of that before, when I was working with Leola and Adeline, but they treated me as the leader of our little trio. I suppose that's partially my fault. But being in situations like this, with you, as equals... it's what I was hoping for when I started doing this nonsense."

Dorothy chuckled. "I have to agree with you on that. Although I would prefer to be drier next time."

"Yes, that would be ideal. Do you have the torch?"

Dorothy retrieved it from her pack and switched it on. She swept the area and moved forward to shine it into the tunnel. They had compared notes while they were still on the surface, combining what each version of Neville had told them to get a complete idea of what they might be facing. Unfortunately neither account was particularly enlightening about the underground portion of his journey.

"Once more unto the breach?"

Trafalgar grunted. "Perhaps our rallying cry shouldn't be part of a speech which mentions 'English dead'."

"Hm, good point. Nothing else comes to mind, so let's just... go."

Felix no longer looked like himself. Or rather, he didn't look like the man she met a few days earlier. He looked like that man's brother, vaguely familiar but also not. The Felix Neville she'd met had been clean-shaven but this man had a beard. He was wearing different clothing, and there was the pink scar tissue of an old burn under the collar of his shirt. He'd been unconscious since their arrival at the lake, but he woke as they moved him to lean against a tree next to the concussed man Dorothy had introduced as Mr. Ketcham. Felix sat silently, swiveling his head back and forth to take in his surroundings.

Rute had quickly taken command of the men who were still capable of putting up a defense. They were currently establishing a perimeter to make sure the natives wouldn't attack them again. She was tending to Ketcham's wounds when she became aware of Felix staring at her. It was peculiar. She felt as if she'd built up a rapport with the man, but now he was regarding her like they'd never met.

"How are you feeling, Captain?"

"Your name is Cora, isn't it? Cora... Hart."

"Cora Hyde," she said with an understanding smile. "I'll try not to be very offended. You have been referring to me by my given name, so it makes sense that the other might slip your mind."

He grunted softly and looked at the water again. "You're like someone I once knew in a dream. Or the other part was a dream, and I'm..." He squeezed his eyes shut and pinched the bridge of his nose. "There was an airplane. Massive and marvelous, unlike nothing I've ever seen. Splendid even in decay. Was that real? You and I, we stood in that plane. I tied you to a chair."

"Afraid not," she said.

"God damn my brain," he whispered. "I can no longer... I can't know if I'm remembering a memory I lived, or recalling an event that happened to him, or just remembering a dream. I only know exactly what I'm looking at now, and even that seems to be through a haze."

Cora put a canteen in his hands and helped him take a drink. "Something definitely happened to you, Captain Neville. Something none of us have ever seen or could have prepared for. It's bound to be traumatic. Soon we'll be out of this forest and back to civilization where you can recover in peace and safety."

He lowered his head. "I pray you never have to feel this... uncertainty."

"I... actually have felt something similar, I think. I spent a while in a sanitarium. By choice, I assure you. I couldn't trust my mind or my actions, and I had fallen into a deep depression. I worried I might harm myself just to silence the storm behind my eyes. I don't know if that unsettled feeling will ever completely go away. But I'm learning to accept it as part of me. For better or worse."

Neville looked up and met her gaze. "Thank you."

"You're welcome. For now, rest."

She patted his arm and stood. She walked to the shore and focused on the point where the lake became a waterfall. The plan, established before Dorothy and Trafalgar disappeared over the edge and began their slow descent, was they would have ninety minutes to explore. At the end of that time, Cora would try to make contact with them. If they didn't answer, she was supposed to gather everyone and head back to safety. Whether that meant the camp she and Trafalgar remembered or the airplane wreckage Dorothy had come from, no one could say.

Cora stared at the cave entrance and tried not to think of another dark scar in rocky ground. An island in the Mediterranean, a beast she had never seen but felt deep in her bones. It elicited a feeling of sheer, primal terror in the unevolved part of her brain. It was the part of humanity that never quite left the forest, the part that let her see the movement of a spider from the corner of her eye or woke her in the middle of the night because there'd been a strange sound.

She'd lost people the last time she saw a cave like this. She didn't know what happened to them, if they had died quickly or in terror, and that knowledge haunted her. She swore this time it would be different. No matter what happened here, she would not leave Dorothy or Trafalgar in the dark unknown.

Trafalgar was tasked with keeping an eye on the time, since Dorothy couldn't be trusted to check her watch with any regularity in a situation like this. Climbing down the wall had taken twenty-three minutes of their exploration time. They had been following the Pratear for nearly ten minutes now. It stretched the width of the tunnel, which meant their boots and pants-legs were soaked. She wasn't looking forward to a day-long trek back to camp in that condition.

Ahead of her, Dorothy held up her hand. They both stopped, and

Trafalgar tilted her head so she could listen for whatever Dorothy had heard. Water lapped against stone and the echo was almost musical. She was about to give up when the sound came again. A slap, louder than a wave would make against the stone walls, followed by a long sliding noise.

"That's not a good sound," Dorothy whispered.

"I can't say whether it's good or bad," Trafalgar said, matching her volume, "but it doesn't exactly encourage me to continue forward."

Dorothy said, "We could go back..."

Trafalgar shook her head. "Whatever is happening, it started down here. We have to continue forward. Would you like me to take the lead?"

"Don't be ridiculous." She faced forward again. "With this echo, that sound was just as likely to have come from behind us."

"Comforting..."

"Keep your eyes open, Miss Trafalgar."

They started moving again. "In the spirit of taking our minds off whatever that noise may have been, I want you to know I am not offended."

"Pardon?"

"I was very emotionally vulnerable with you on the wall. I admitted that I feared you were lost forever and how that made me feel. But you didn't reciprocate. You probably had some uncertainty as to my fate, and Cora's. You could have expressed some relief at the discovery we had survived the attack."

Dorothy stopped walking but didn't turn around.

"Did you hear something else?"

"No. I..." Her voice was soft, and her head was turned away from the torch so her face was in shadow. "I didn't let myself dwell on it. The possibility of repeating what happened with Desmond. That I had led two more people I care greatly for into danger. And to once again survive when they didn't. I refused to carry that weight in the middle of a mission."

Trafalgar felt ashamed for making light. "Dorothy, I didn't intend..."

Dorothy turned around. Her brow was furrowed, her eyes still hidden in the darkness. "When we walked into the clearing by the lake, I wasn't sure what I was seeing. In one eye, the water was calm, but in the other I could see people thrashing. The tribesmen were like phantoms. I saw you." Her voice broke. "Near the edge. About to fall. Just like Desmond. And I... I didn't know if what I was seeing was real or illusion. I knew that if I threw myself into the water to grab you, and you weren't really there, I would be throwing myself to my death. But I thought it was worth the risk."

"How do I respond to that?" Trafalgar asked.

"You don't." Dorothy swept her hand over her face and looked away. "I know you were only teasing me. But I would have let it go unsaid without being prompted, and I'm grateful you gave me the opening to say those things. They very much needed to be said."

"Thank you. And if I didn't say it before, thank you for saving my life."

"It was my pleasure to do so."

When they began moving again, Trafalgar noticed the water seemed more sluggish than before. She hadn't been bothering to lift her foot entirely with each step since it was easier to just slide it along the bottom, but now there was more resistance against her calves. She aimed her torch down and illuminated the flowing black surface. It looked more like oil than water, though the way it was breaking around her legs was—

It took her a moment to realize what she was actually seeing, and her blood ran cold. "Dorothy, stop."

"What's wrong?"

"Can you move to the edge of the water? Get back on solid ground?"

Dorothy looked at Trafalgar, then aimed her torch at her own feet. "Good lord!"

"No sudden movements," Trafalgar said as calmly as possible.

"Snakes?" Dorothy asked. There seemed to be more snakes than water in the river at the moment, their scaly bodies rolling and writhing against each other.

"So it would seem." Her heart beat a rapid rhythm against her ribs. She tried to swallow, but her mouth was dry. "I'm not terribly fond of snakes."

Dorothy said, "The majority of species are entirely harmless to humans."

"That cannot possibly be true."

"I choose to believe it at the moment."

"Fair enough." Trafalgar shone her light at the wall. There was no ledge in this part of the cavern where they could get away from the slithering beasts. Moving the beam higher, she saw nothing on the walls they could grab to lift themselves up. "I have a horrible suggestion."

Dorothy whimpered. "I know what you're going to suggest. I don't like it."

"I know. But we have no idea when exactly the snakes began this little migration. They haven't done anything to us yet. Much as you choose to believe they're harmless, I choose to believe they'll ignore us if we don't do anything to draw their ire."

"I told you I wouldn't like it."

"Courage, Lady Boone." She tried to make herself sound more confident than she was. "Captain Neville and his *men* made this same journey. Certainly you don't plan to turn around and go back now, proving once and for all that women have no place doing this sort of thing."

Dorothy said, "That was lousy."

"But did it work?"

"Of course it worked, damn you."

Moving forward was more difficult now that she knew what she was walking through, but she tried her best to ignore it. Sweat broke out on her forehead and upper lip as she anticipated being bitten with every step. She was grateful that her boots extended past the cuffs of her pants, so there was little chance of anything slithering underneath against her skin. She placed her feet carefully and tried not to step on any tails.

The snakes, for their part, didn't seem particularly interested in them. She could now hear the subtle hissing she'd originally taken for the sound of falling water.

"How many do you suppose there are?"

"That," Trafalgar said, "does not seem like a calming thing to contemplate. I'm more than willing to let it remain a mystery."

"I believe that~" Dorothy stopped suddenly and looked down. "Crumbs. Trafalgar, tense your leg muscles."

"What? Why..." She felt it then. One of the snakes had wrapped itself around her ankle. She felt its head against her calf and the disgusting pressure of its weight as it coiled to rise higher on her leg. She flexed her calf muscles and let the beast wrap tightly around her. Once it reached her knee, she relaxed and felt a gap between her and the snake. She tried to lift her foot out of the loop, but the snake instantly tightened.

"Ahh. Thank you for the warning, but it didn't help. Are you ensnared as well?"

Dorothy said, "I have one on each leg. They're up to my knee. I can't move."

Trafalgar unsheathed her knife. There was no way to cut at the snakes without cutting herself, but if she could wedge the blade between its skin and her leg...

"Damn! I don't recommend getting your hands close to the bloody faces."

"Were you bitten?"

"Very nearly."

Trafalgar was about to suggest another plan of attack when she was stopped by an unfamiliar voice which echoed off the sharp edges of the tunnel.

"Cut as many of them as you want. Another will take the place of any you kill. And even if you manage to free yourselves, my children have flooded the path back to the cave entrance. It would take only one bite from one fang to fill you with poison and render you helpless."

Dorothy extended her torch. Its light filled the cavern ahead of them and, at the very edge of its reach, they could see the shadowy outline of their captor.

"Do you greet all your guests in this manner?" Dorothy asked.

"Guests? You're not guests. You're intruders." She stepped closer, revealing she wore a dark cloak with green piping. Her arms were clasped behind her back. "This is how I deal with intruders."

"Had we known this was your home, we would have been more polite about it. Allow me to make amends. I'm Lady Dorothy Boone, of London.

This~"

"Miss Trafalgar of Abyssinia."

Dorothy narrowed her eyes. "Have we met before?"

"We're meeting now. And I remember."

She came closer, revealing a woman much younger than Dorothy expected. She couldn't have been older than mid-twenties, with her black hair hanging loose around her unlined features.

"You will have told me about your friend, the man who remembers time in reverse. He sees the future but forgets the past. I suffer from a similar affliction. I can see... everything. Past. Future. Everything I've seen or will see, playing in my mind like a loop."

"That would drive a person mad," Dorothy said, realizing only on the last word that the other woman was saying the exact same thing at the same time. She blinked in surprise and then said, "You would be a riot at parties." That was echoed as well.

The woman smiled. "I don't get out to many parties, Lady Boone. We have a choice about how we continue forward. You can be bitten by one of my pets, their poison will paralyze you, I'll take you where I need you to be, and wait for the antidote to give you back your limbs. Or you can agree to come with me willingly. I'm patient, so I really haven't got much of an opinion."

Trafalgar said, "If what you are saying is true, then I suppose you know what our answer will be."

A chuckle, and a slow nod. "You are correct, Trafalgar." With no apparent signal or command, the pressure around their legs relaxed and the snakes fell back to rejoin the flow. The woman turned and began to walk. "Follow me."

Dorothy glanced at Trafalgar, who shrugged and started walking.

"It occurs to me," Dorothy said, "that we never told you our names."

"There was no proper introduction," the woman admitted, "but in our time together, I will have had heard your names many times."

Dorothy was stuck on 'will-have-had.' "And since we don't have the benefit of foresight? What might we call you?"

"You may call me D'janira."

Trafalgar said, "Is that actually your name?"

"No. But I like how it will sound coming out of your mouth, Lady Boone."

Dorothy looked at Trafalgar again, apparently looking for some sign she understood their current predicament. Trafalgar could only sigh and shake her head, keeping her torch held high as they followed D'janira into the darkness.

CHAPTER FOURTEEN

EVENTUALLY THE cave began to fill with a sickly green-yellow light. D'janira led them through a crack in the wall that opened into a large open area. Dorothy saw a few flat surfaces draped with furs and others with what appeared to be rudimentary kitchenware. She was very aware of the knife collection in a wooden case that made them look like they were on display. The green light glinted off their blades, proving just how sharp they were. The edges of the room were crowded with crates and trunks which had all suffered some degree of water damage.

D'janira unfastened the buttons of her cloak and slipped it off to reveal a sleeveless white shirt and black slacks. She folded the cloak carefully and hooked it on a high stone so that it could hang without touching the floor.

"You're welcome to share my food and drink. There's not much, but I can be generous."

"I believe we'll pass for the time being."

D'janira smiled. "I know. But it will be there when you're hungry later and go scrounging."

Dorothy tried not to show her discomfort at the woman's prescience. "If what you claim is true, why bother with formalities? You know why we're here, what we want, and you know if we'll be successful in asking for your help. We might as well get it out of the way now."

"Yes." D'janira sighed and looked at the ground. "Things would be much simpler if everyone shared my... affliction, ability, however you may categorize it. I could tell you everything that will happen between us. Bid you farewell. Move on with my day. But you would never be convinced. You would think there's something you didn't say or do. Some tactic you hadn't tried. You won't give up until you've actually made your argument. I can't give you the final piece of a puzzle and expect you to see the entire picture. So it saves time to just let you play it out. As slow and boring as that is from my perspective."

Trafalgar said, "Must be a tedious existence."

"You have no idea."

"So you know that we're here to set things right," Dorothy said.

"No. That's not correct. You're here to discover what went wrong. You want to know what happened when Captain Neville came into the caves and why that visit led to a catastrophe."

Dorothy said, "I suppose that's accurate. Whatever happened created a ripple effect and will eventually cause an airplane to be sent into the past. I assume from your unique relationship with time that you have some idea about what happened."

"I do." She walked to one of the flat surfaces and leaned against it. "There is something in this cave. Something special, powerful. It was what granted my unique perspective. It is my duty to watch over it, to defend it from people like your Captain Neville. He came to this forest in search of a river which could turn anything to silver. What he found was far more valuable."

Trafalgar said, "A window to the future."

D'janira nodded slowly, her eyes distant. "He was in an unusual position. If my claims were true, it was an invaluable resource. But he needed to find a way to trick me so he could use it for his own gain. But if tricking me was possible, then the skill must be flawed, and therefore less valuable. I told him every step he would take, every scheme he would attempt, and still he wouldn't give up. I could sense his desperation growing and I knew that eventually he or his men would turn violent. So I told them that drinking from the Pratear would grant them the same knowledge."

"And that is how he lost his memory?" Dorothy said.

"Exactly. I made sure he only drank a small amount. Drinking too much could have eradicated his entire recollection down to childhood. Once he'd consumed it, I guided his men out of the caves and sent them on their way."

Dorothy tilted her head to one side, curious. "But if you know everything, past to future, you must have known he wouldn't be convinced."

"I knew he would come back, and that he would be too weak to return. I knew he would send the two of you into the cave instead of returning himself."

"And this was an outcome you wanted?"

D'janira shrugged. "It was the outcome which was guaranteed by the set of events I had put in motion."

Trafalgar held up her hand. "Wait. You're speaking as if the future is a concrete fact. We've spent the past few days in separate timelines. Dorothy was briefly held captive in an airplane which, from my perspective, doesn't exist. That implies time is fluid, the future and even the present are unwritten and can be changed."

"Yes."

Dorothy furrowed her brow. "Which?"

"Both." D'janira smiled and raised an eyebrow. "Now you understand my curse even better than before. Just because I know what's going to happen doesn't always mean it will. I told Captain Neville which scheme he would try, which made him devise a new one. I outlined that for him as well, because it was the new version of events. And so on."

"So things set in stone can be changed." Dorothy thought about that for a moment, then drew her pistol. She aimed it at D'janira's head. "Say I pull the trigger."

D'janira said, "I know you won't, because that isn't the kind of person you are. But I can also see a scenario in which you attempt to fire that gun only to discover it's waterlogged from the dunking you took earlier."

Dorothy kept the gun steady for another moment before she lowered it. "But the point remains that we can change the future. We can affect the past and, in doing so, create a new future."

"No."

Trafalgar pressed two fingers against her forehead. "I'm very confused."

"Every future that can exist does exist. One path within a maze doesn't cease to exist just because you went a different way. Every turn is still there. Most people exist inside the maze and only see their immediate surroundings. I can see the maze from above."

"You see the dead ends," Dorothy said.

D'janira shook her head. "There are no dead ends in this maze. Only new mazes and different paths. Sometimes they lead to the same destination, sometimes they lead somewhere completely new. At the moment, what we're experiencing, is a shattering of the walls. One path bleeds into the next. Chaos."

"Okay." Dorothy began to pace. "Let's deal with the facts. Something Neville did while he was down here caused the anomaly which grows for fifty years until it's large enough for Ackon Air Flight 372 to pass through. We don't need to understand it, we just need to know what he did and how to stop it while there's still time."

"That's not what you're here to do."

Trafalgar said, "We came to this forest to find Captain Neville and his men. Our mission evolved when we found out why he went missing last year."

"It's evolved again," D'janira said. "The Burnt Empire is coming for the Pratear. They want it for the same reason your Captain Neville did. I've seen their attack, and I've seen you defending this place against it. That's why you're here."

"And if we're successful, the... the..." She waved her hand above her head to indicate the surface. "Things will go back to normal?"

D'janira said, "Things will be as they should be."

"I don't like that answer," Dorothy muttered, "but I suppose I'll have to be satisfied with it. There's really no way we could surprise you, is there?"

"No." D'janira smiled sadly. "Being surprised is a small pleasure that everyone takes for granted. I know that you'll want to talk about this privately, without me lurking, and night has fallen. So I'll take my leave." She gestured to an opening in the wall that, upon closer inspection, was indeed artificially-created rather than naturally-formed. "You may spend the night there. You'll find connecting chambers with food storage and a restroom. There's also clothing so you can change out of these wet things. I bid you a good night. We'll speak again in the morning."

Dorothy said, "We could leave right now. Go back the way we came, climb back up to the surface."

"I don't believe you will. You're close to your goal, Lady Boone. And neither of you is the sort to walk away when confronted with something this... unique. Besides..." She turned and offered a smile that Dorothy couldn't quite classify. "The snakes are still out there in the dark. Sleep well, ladies."

She vanished through an opening in the wall.

Dorothy looked at Trafalgar. "I can't tell if we've just been threatened or warned."

"In the past," Trafalgar said, "if there's any doubt, I've found it's wiser to assume threat. Cora and the others will be worried about us."

"Right. But I have the feeling any attempt to go back, even to let them know we're safe, would be met with serpentine interference." Trafalgar nodded her agreement. Dorothy sighed and looked down at herself. Their clothes had started to dry, leaving her feeling as if she was wearing a burlap sack. "So. To bed, I suppose."

"And save the world in the morning."

Dorothy grinned. "Yes. Always."

Cora thought the jungle was foreboding during the day. But night was a completely different beast.

The first evening, when Trafalgar was still recovering from her brief illness, Cora almost had a panic attack when the sun began setting. The darkness was so utterly complete it was as if the world was being erased. The animal noises she'd been unaware of hearing all day vanished so suddenly that the silence was almost a new sound. Felix had comforted her, the first act of kindness he'd shown her and a cornerstone of trust.

Of course now she couldn't hold onto that trust. She sat with her back against a stone and looked at him, Captain Felix Neville. She barely recognized him. He still hadn't regained consciousness, which was worrisome. But he had only a mild fever and occasionally muttered in his sleep, so there was definitely life behind his closed eyes.

Ketcham, the man who had appeared with Dorothy, was doing much better with his recovery. He'd woken up not long after Dorothy and Trafalgar entered the cave and expressed his disappointment at not being invited loudly and with inventive cursing. At the moment he was sitting next to the fire Cora had helped build, poking a stick into the embers.

Rute, the frightening soldier-ish woman who was also from Dorothy's party, returned to the group without announcing her approach. She was like a spirit, seemingly moving through the foliage without disturbing a single leaf. She made Cora's flesh crawl.

"Anything out there we should be worried about?" Cora asked.

"If there was, I eliminated it." Rute stopped in front of the fire. She removed a bloody kerchief from her pocket, unwrapped it, and speared whatever it was on a stick. She crouched and extended the slice of meat into the flame. "Any word from down below?"

Cora was transfixed by the glistening meat. She prayed it had been an animal. She was concerned that she couldn't discount the possibility it was one of the tribesmen they'd fought off earlier.

"No, nothing," she finally said.

"That's not a good sign. How long are we supposed to wait before we go down there, guns blazing?"

Cora said, "This is Lady Boone and Miss Trafalgar. We have to trust them."

Ketcham grunted. "No offense, lady, but my experience with those two has been less than stellar. Boone almost got herself trampled and the other one nearly fell into the cave flailing around with one of those tribesmen. Their reputation is sounding more and more like carnival barking."

"Trust me," Cora said, "these two have a way of getting thing done. It may not be pretty, but they get results. We stay here. We wait. Until we're given reason to move."

"Like those wild men in the woods?" Ketcham said.

Rute checked the skin of her meat. "We shouldn't have to worry about them tonight. I tracked them for a mile, and there's no sign of doubling back. They went home to wherever they came from."

"You'll forgive me for not sleeping tonight."

"Suit yourself." Rute took a bite of her meal.

Cora looked at Felix, who shifted in his sleep. His brow was furrowed but he seemed to be more at peace than the rest of them. She envied him. She also envied Trafalgar and Boone. She didn't know what they had found or what horrors they might have been facing, but it had to be better than sitting in the dark surrounded by unseen beasts and hostile compatriots.

She leaned against her stone, drew her knees up to her chest, and closed her eyes in the hopes she could trick her brain into shutting down to give her a little rest.

CHAPTER FIFTEEN

THE CHAMBERS they'd been given had four stone beds with thick pelts folded on top to serve as bedding. Two racks of clothing stood on opposite sides of the room. Dorothy went to one and Trafalgar to the other. They checked the outfits, looked at each other, and crossed in the center of the room to trade sides. Dorothy had no idea where D'janira had acquired these things, but they all seemed to be very fine material and carefully stitched.

"You don't suppose she made all of this herself, do you?" Dorothy asked.

"Did she strike you as the type who spends her free time as a seamstress?"

Dorothy smiled. "Not exactly, no. But I also can't see her wandering the aisles of Marks and Spencer with a list of our sizes, either."

"You saw those trunks and crates in the main room. These things probably came from crates that fell off boats and drifted upriver." She pulled out a man's shirt which had been slashed across the chest and neatly repaired. "Or from unlucky adventurers who crossed the locals. But perhaps she did make these herself. We have no idea where she came from. Whoever this D'janira is, she's certainly led an interesting life."

"True."

Dorothy glanced over her shoulder to see Trafalgar was already disrobing. She started to look away, but her eye was caught by an M-shaped scar on Trafalgar's right shoulder. There was another on the left shoulder, older and more faded. She moved closer without thinking, without being fully aware of crossing the space. Trafalgar had taken a tunic off the rack but sensed Dorothy's approach and looked at her, holding the cloth against her chest.

"My god." Dorothy could see more marks up close. Little scratches, longer cuts, some that had been treated medically and others which had obviously been left to heal on their own. They were the results of falling, rolling, being in the way of dropped things, and other hazards of their profession.

Trafalgar said, "I'm sure your back looks similar."

"Yes," Dorothy admitted. "But it's easy to ignore those. Easy to forget just how many of them there are."

She lightly touched one of Trafalgar's scars with her middle finger. Trafalgar tensed but didn't pull away. Dorothy moved her finger and gooseflesh erupted in her wake. Her lips quirked in a meager smile, but she was too intently focused on what she was doing to be distracted. The scar ended but her finger continued, up to the soft skin of Trafalgar's neck where her hair had once rested. She spread her hand out and let it span across the curve of her shoulder.

"We're more than the sum of our scars," Dorothy whispered.

Trafalgar looked at her again. The silence between them in that moment was as heavy as any words they could have said. Dorothy thought of how close they'd both come to dying. Sure, they had faced death before. Dorothy had actually drowned on one of their missions. But this time... Dorothy moved her hand to Trafalgar's cheek, and Trafalgar finally turned so they were facing each other.

"You scolded me about not having a reaction to the fact you were alive. The truth is, I refused to let myself believe you were dead because... If I let myself think I'd lost you so soon after losing Desmond... I don't think I would have survived that. No one else knows what this life is like. Not even Beatrice really understands. Not the way you do."

Trafalgar took a deep breath and let it out slowly.

Dorothy's hand had slipped off the shoulder to her bicep, and now she moved it to Trafalgar's cheek. She leaned in, the difference in their heights becoming an issue for the first time as Dorothy pressed her lips to the corner of Trafalgar's mouth. It could have remained a friendly kiss, affection between close colleagues, until Trafalgar turned her head, and Dorothy touched her tongue to lips that parted under that slight pressure.

There was no heat of the moment to blame, no adrenaline rush or life-saving gambit to celebrate. It was a premeditated choice on both their parts that still managed to feel spontaneous and unexpected. Trafalgar let go of the tunic she'd been holding and brought her hands up. She lightly brushed either side of Dorothy's face before dropping her hands lower to touch the collar of her shirt. Her fingers plucked at the button, not quite getting it undone.

"What are we doing?" Her voice was barely louder than a gasp.

Dorothy put her hands on top of Trafalgar's. "This," she said, and kissed her again.

Trafalgar opened one button and after that, the rest of them went easily. Dorothy was aware her skin was clammy from wearing her wet clothes for so long, but Trafalgar ignored that as she slipped her hand under the material. Dorothy followed the curve of Trafalgar's flanks with both hands until she found the waistband of her pants. She twisted the button and pushed them down, and Trafalgar let them fall. Her underwear went next. She stepped out of the material, putting her weight against Dorothy, forcing her to take a rapid series of steps backward toward the beds.

"What about D'janira?" Dorothy said against Trafalgar's cheek. She was very aware of the fact this chamber didn't have any sort of door.

"If we believe her claims," Trafalgar said as her hand moved down the bodice of Dorothy's underclothes, "she already knows what does or doesn't happen tonight. So there's... no reason to cease for fear of being discovered."

"Reasonable."

Dorothy took a step back, one hand on Trafalgar's hip, and finally took in the sight of the other woman's nudity. She unconsciously swept her tongue across her bottom lip as her eyes trailed over the curves, up to her breasts. She finally met Trafalgar's gaze once more and held it as she shrugged out of her blouse. Trafalgar's jaw was tight. She held her body very still as Dorothy's shirt was discarded. Her belt buckle jingled as it came loose.

Trafalgar smiled at the sight of Dorothy's underwear. She teased the string tied into a bow under the hem of the camisole.

"Men's shorts?"

"My shorts," Dorothy said. Her voice sounded uncharacteristically meek to her own ears. "Men prefer union suits. These are being sold, so someone might as well take advantage of them. Do you like them?"

Trafalgar said, "Oh, yes. I like them very much." Her forefinger curled though the bow and pulled. Dorothy let them fall, holding her breath until she stepped out of them. She crossed her arms, grabbed the camisole with both hands, and pulled it over her head. The speed of removing it caused her breasts to sway a bit, and Trafalgar seemed briefly hypnotized by the movement.

"Wow," she said.

"I know." Dorothy smiled. "Freckles."

Trafalgar said, "What? Oh... yes. But... yes. May I... should..."

"I very much hope you will."

She closed her eyes when Trafalgar's hand cupped her breast, the thumb sweeping across the nipple. Trafalgar put her other hand on the back of Dorothy's head and drew her in for another kiss, taking charge this time as she explored with her fingertips.

"I don't know what I'm doing," Trafalgar said.

"Then you're doing a fantastic job of guessing."

Trafalgar said, "Don't make light. I've never... with..."

"Ah. You'd like me to teach you. How to touch me. How to please me?"

Another deep exhale. "Yes."

Dorothy kissed her and stepped back. She felt the edge of the bed against her thighs and sat down. She spread her legs and urged Trafalgar to kneel between them with gentle pressure on her shoulder. She moved her hand to the back of Trafalgar's head and brought the other hand to her mouth. She wet the fingers, never breaking eye contact as she put that hand between her legs.

"Pay attention," she said.

"To what?" Trafalgar's eyes roamed Dorothy's body, lingering on her breasts but frequently venturing lower. "It's all... I... you're beautiful, Lady Boone."

"And you're magnificent," Dorothy said. "My hand, Miss Trafalgar. Watch my hand."

Trafalgar stared.

Breathless, Dorothy said, "Do you see what I'm doing? With this finger... these fingers...?" Her face was burning. "Watch. Like this... gently. Taking my time."

"Teasing."

"Yes. No rush. No need to rush." She swallowed. "Touch yourself like this."

Trafalgar's hands were resting on Dorothy's thighs, but she moved one between her own legs.

"That's good. Like that. Do you often do this?"

"Rarely," Trafalgar said. "When... the need arises..."

Dorothy said, "I do it whenever I can. It feels magnificent. Why deprive myself of... such joy? A simple pleasure inflicted on myself in the privacy of my bedroom. Of course it's a different thing entirely when there's an audience. Do you like watching?"

"Very much," Trafalgar said. "I've often wondered. Imagined."

"Fantasized?"

Trafalgar looked up into Dorothy's eyes before quickly returning focus. "Sometimes. You are a beautiful woman. Sensuous. It's hard not to imagine you in bed. With women."

"I like that you've thought about me. I've thought about you as well." She wet her lips and closed her eyes. "It's so rare to meet a woman taller than me. We're usually equal heights. You are magnificently tall. I want to feel your arms around me. I want to lay my cheek on your breast while sweat cools on my forehead while~"

"Dorothy..." Trafalgar threw herself forward, capturing Dorothy's lips and pushing her back onto the furs. Dorothy wrapped her legs around Trafalgar's waist. They crossed arms, groping for each other. Trafalgar grasped as Dorothy found her target, then bared her teeth as her own fingers brushed against slick skin.

"Like this," Dorothy whispered, or perhaps it was 'I like this,' even she wasn't certain. She was too distracted by Trafalgar's weight, her hip between her legs to push her hand harder against Dorothy's mound.

They broke the kiss for quiet gasps, moans, and to implore each other in short, simple directives: "Harder" or "there" or "more." Dorothy put her free hand in the small of Trafalgar's back, just above her ass, and pushed, setting a rhythm for her to begin thrusting. She squeezed her eyes shut and moved her head to bite Trafalgar's shoulder, hoping to muffle her voice. She was only capable of noises now, jaw wide, tongue pressed against sweaty skin, teeth digging in just enough to leave marks that would last a few minutes after they finished.

"Dorothy." It reached her ear like a desperate grunt, echoed a moment later. "Dorothy." And again on each forward thrust, punctuated by Trafalgar's thumb on her clit, two fingers inside of her. Dorothy felt Trafalgar's muscles clenching around her own fingers and knew the end was near. She relaxed her jaw and turned the bite into a kiss, pressing her lips against the throbbing vein in Trafalgar's throat.

"Let yourself go for me," she whispered, and Trafalgar cried out. She arched her back, rising up, and Dorothy pressed her face into the hollow between her hanging breasts. Trafalgar's convulsions set off Dorothy's own orgasm. She held tightly, her heels digging into the stone bed. Their moaning was uncoordinated but their bodies moved as one. Dorothy fell back, pulling Trafalgar with her.

"I finished," Trafalgar said.

"You did?" Dorothy said. "When?"

Trafalgar laughed and dropped her hand on top of Dorothy's face. Dorothy angled her neck until she could get two of the fingers into her mouth to taste herself off of them. Trafalgar made the hissing noise Dorothy now recognized as a sign of acute arousal. She brought her own hand up, and Trafalgar tentatively kissed the tips of them.

"Odd."

Dorothy popped the fingers into her mouth and smacked her lips. "Mm. But a very good odd."

Trafalgar kissed Dorothy high on the cheek, just below her eye. They were both out of breath, weak-kneed, and Trafalgar repositioned herself so she could settle on top of Dorothy. Their lips met in a casual, idle, slow kiss. When Dorothy inhaled, she felt Trafalgar's stomach slipping against hers. Trafalgar's thigh was a strong pressure between hers. She found Trafalgar's hand, linked their fingers, and squeezed. Trafalgar rolled to one side and pulled Dorothy with her, holding her tightly. She put one hand on the back of Dorothy's head to guide it to her breast.

"Is this how you fantasized?"

Dorothy smiled and kissed the curve of sweaty skin in front of her mouth. One dark nipple, still erect, was close enough for her to flick it with her tongue.

"I've never been creative enough to imagine something like this," Dorothy said.

Trafalgar threaded Dorothy's hair with her fingers. "I... When we get back to London, I hope this doesn't complicate things with Beatrice."

"We have an understanding."

"I know, yes, with people you encounter out in the world. People you leave when you come home. I imagine it will be different with someone who lives under the same roof."

Dorothy shook her head. "I don't believe she'll care. But we'll discuss it. We can be mature adults about it. And now that it's happened, I think we can all admit that this was bound to happen eventually."

"We can?" Trafalgar said. "I admit, my feelings for you have been confusing lately. But to go so far as to call it inevitable..."

Dorothy sat up and put her chin on Trafalgar's breast. "I knew. Even when I hated you, I could admit you were a beautiful woman. I couldn't imagine becoming your friend first, but I did always feel a physical attraction to you."

Trafalgar raised an eyebrow. "I see. Dorothy...?"

"Yes?"

"Your chin is very sharp."

Dorothy laughed and kissed the spot where it had been pressing. "Better?"

"Very much."

Dorothy put her head down and closed her eyes. Trafalgar's fingers in her hair was very calming. She felt like they should sit up for a while, discuss D'janira and the Burnt Empire attack she claimed was imminent. They needed to strategize. But it had been such a demanding day, and she was so utterly exhausted, and Trafalgar's touch was so comforting... She felt safe and her mind was quiet. So she kept her eyes closed and just let herself slip into a restful sleep.

CHAPTER SIXTEEN

"I'M HAVING difficulty with something..."

Cora was mostly talking to herself, her voice barely more than a mutter, but it carried to Ketcham a few yards away. He held up his canteen.

"The granola? It's easier to break off a piece with your fingers, pop it in your mouth, then drown it with a big drink of water. It's the only way to get it down."

"What?" She looked at the granola in her hand. "Oh. No. I've eaten enough of this garbage that I barely even notice it anymore. There's something..." She scanned the area around the lake. "Last night when we arrived, when Captain Neville lost consciousness and you came out of nowhere with Lady Boone... there were... men with us."

Ketcham pondered that. "British?"

"No. These were natives. They were members of the Ru... Uru... something tribe." She closed her eyes and tried to remember. "One was named... Matthew."

"A member of a local tribe named after a Christian prophet?" He chuckled. "I find that very unlikely."

"Matta?" she said under her breath, but it didn't sound right, either. The sharp edges of her memory were becoming blurry. She and Trafalgar had been saved by Captain Neville. They traveled through the forest to... a safe place, where she helped nurse Trafalgar back to health. There had been people in that place. Or... now she wasn't certain. It was like telling the details of a dream hours after waking up. She couldn't see faces or hear voices. Maybe it had just been her and Felix in the wilds.

Ketcham said, "For what it's worth, you and Trafalgar were alone when we found you. I'm sure Rute can confirm that when she gets back."

"Yes, and when might that be?" She scanned the trees. The sun had risen enough to brighten the general area, but there was no sign of the brutish woman.

"She keeps her own schedule. Like your friends seem to." He grimaced as he swallowed another chunk of granola. "It's morning. Surely they would've made contact by now if it was possible. Clearly something happened to them. We should retreat somewhere safe and consider our options."

Cora said, "No. We wait until midday. If we don't receive some sign of life by then, we'll go into the caves ourselves." She had walked away from one team lost underground, and she wasn't about to repeat that sin. "Besides, we can't go anywhere with Captain Neville still unconscious."

Rute chose that moment to rejoin them. "I'm not dragging him. It was bad enough I had to carry him." She nodded at Ketcham as she passed them on her way to the lake.

"That was *your* fault," Ketcham said. "If you hadn't knocked me out..."

She crouched and dipped her hand into the water, then dragged her palm down over her face. "Burnt Empire folk seem to be nocturnal. I stopped hearing them toward dawn. Once the sun came up, it was like they were ghosts."

"Speaking of ghosts," Cora said, "do you recall if, when you met us last night, Trafalgar and I were accompanied by two men?"

"Matta and Viejas," Rute said without hesitation. She paused and tilted her head to the side. "No. Wait, that's... what wasn't you, was it...?"

Cora said, "Those names do sound familiar..."

"I might be remembering a different expedition." Rute didn't sound certain, but she stood and walked to Neville. They had wrapped him in a blanket and given him one of their packs for a pillow. "We need to wake him up."

"We don't know what happened to him. His mind may be damaged. If we wake him before he's ready~"

"If we wait until he's ready, he might get killed in his sleep because he's not able to run."

Cora sighed. "We wait until midday, then we venture into the caves. We owe that to Dorothy and Trafalgar."

"I'll go," Rute said. "You can stay here with~"

"No." Cora's voice was stronger than she could remember ever making it in the past. Even Rute seemed taken aback. "I'm finished with sending people into the unknown dark while I cower safely above. When the time comes, I'm going."

Rute nodded slowly. She was looking at Cora differently, as if truly seeing her for the first time. Cora knew she came off as studious, but she went into the field as much as Dorothy and Trafalgar before sidelining herself. This mission was exactly what she needed to reconstitute her former backbone. She just hoped it didn't prove disastrous for her friends.

They fell asleep facing each other in the same bed, lying on top of the furs. At some point during the night, Trafalgar heard Dorothy say her name but she didn't respond. After a moment, Dorothy kissed the corner of her mouth and pulled away from her. Trafalgar let her go. When she woke again, she rolled over to find Dorothy already dressed and sitting on the other bed. The clothes were very basic - a V-neck tunic and diaphanous slacks - but Dorothy looked magnificent in them.

"Is it morning?" Trafalgar asked.

"Probably close enough." Dorothy looked at her and seemed to make a point of not looking away from her nudity. Her gaze drifted over Trafalgar's chest, to her thighs, and then back up toward her face. "How did you sleep?"

"Very well. You?"

"Not at all. But it's fine. Hardly my first sleepless night."

Trafalgar sat up and gathered the furs around her shoulders. "Sleepless due to the timeline problem, the Burnt Empire, or because of what happened between us?"

"All of the above. Yesterday was an extremely full day."

"It definitely was, yes." Trafalgar wet her lips. "If you're worried that this will affect you and Beatrice's relationship--"

Dorothy said, "No, no, that's not it at all. Trix and I are solid. I'm concerned about you."

"Me?"

"You've never expressed a romantic interest in women before. You've never spoken about it. After the adrenaline wore off, I began to fear that I'd... that my... enthusiasm... combined with the dire situation might have pushed you into doing something you weren't comfortable with. I wanted to ask you again once the emotions faded and the rush had time to wear off."

Trafalgar got up and sat next to Dorothy. "When it comes to romance, you and Beatrice are exclusively interested in women. Desmond was the other end of the spectrum. It seems as if most people in London have a very strict opinion of who they wish to be with regardless of circumstance. I've never wasted much time on that sort of thing. I was approached by men and I returned the attention of those that intrigued me. Then I met you. I saw the possibilities. And the more I got to know you, the more I found myself curious. I'm grateful for what we shared last night. I wouldn't have wanted to share that with anybody else. I hope it can happen again in the future."

Dorothy put her hand on Trafalgar's. "Me too. And I hope you find someone like Beatrice."

"I don't know if it will be easier now that I know more about what I'm looking for, or more difficult now that my options have literally doubled.

But I think I shall enjoy myself on the search."

"And excellent point of view to have." She leaned in and kissed Trafalgar's cheek, then shifted to her lips for a nearly-chaste kiss.

"I have to admit," Dorothy said, "it was a unique experience for me as well. I've never been with anyone who was bald. I never realized how much I like grabbing a handful of my lover's hair."

"Damn. I finally regret the decision."

Dorothy chuckled. "Don't grow it back on my account. You look very debonair."

"I would have to agree with that assessment." D'janira's voice echoed off the stone as she stepped into the room. She wore a cloak similar to the one she'd been wearing when they met, but it was loose to reveal her chest was wrapped in what looked like thick layers of gauze. "I trust you spent the time since we last spoke thinking about my request."

Dorothy looked at Trafalgar, who gave a slight nod. She would go along with whatever Dorothy said in this moment.

"It seems to us that we have little choice but to help. We cannot allow the Burnt Empire to spread to the civilized world. Ideally, we would want to stop them from affecting history, but if we must fight them, then we won't walk away."

"Fantastic. I'll give you the chance to finish dressing." She turned to indicate the door. "Follow this passage. Breakfast will be waiting for you when you're ready, and we can discuss a plan of attack."

Trafalgar dressed, and they left the room together. The sound of running water had been present from the moment they descended into the caves, and they'd both long since stopped thinking about it. But as they moved deeper into the labyrinth of rooms, the sound was almost deafening. The volume was explained when they emerged into what could only be described as a naturally-formed cathedral filled with a crystal-clear lake. It was fed by a dozen waterfalls pouring out of cracks and holes in the domed walls. The surface of the lake was broken at random intervals by broken plinths which were wide enough to serve as stepping stones.

In the center of the lake was a platform which was wider than any of the other stones. D'janira was sitting upon it with her legs crossed in front of her, cloak removed to reveal her bare arms.

"Welcome to the heart of the Pratear." Her voice reverberated off the water and stone. It took several seconds for the echo to fade completely.

"It's... lovely." Dorothy stepped forward, cautious. "This is what we're meant to protect from the Burnt Empire?"

D'janira nodded. Her movements were slow, almost as if she was drugged. "This is what they seek, what will give them the power necessary to dominate your world the way they've dominated the forest. That cannot be allowed to happen."

"We're willing to help you defend this place. If you let us go back to the surface, we can enlist our friends to help us."

"They've been lost to us."

Dorothy tensed. "I beg your pardon?"

"The anomaly you came to prevent has grown stronger. The friends you left behind no longer exist in this particular history. If you returned to the surface, you would find no sign of them."

"That can't be," Trafalgar said. "We remember them!"

D'janira said, "This place exists separately from the outside world. You will remember history as it was until you leave."

"I'm getting half-sick of this entire thing," Dorothy muttered, hand to her forehead. "Navigating timelines and history... it's madness." She sighed and composed herself. "Everything that's going wrong began here. You said this is the heart of the river."

"Felix Neville found this place. He could sense its power. He tried to take it."

Trafalgar was closest to the entrance. She could hear movement behind them and turned so she could see the corridor from the corner of her eye.

Dorothy was scanning the room for anything that seemed mystical. All she saw was water and stone. "There must have been something that contained the power of the Pratear. He must have taken it or destroyed it."

Trafalgar said, "Dorothy..."

"I hear it now," she said. The sound of falling water had been joined by a chorus of hissing. Dorothy moved to the edge of the water, not taking her eyes off D'janira. "You aren't the protector of this place. The snakes are. And you're what they're protecting. The water has some amount of magic, but that's not the important part of the equation. That's just a side effect caused by the fact you live here. You're what the Burnt Empire is coming to steal."

"They always believed the river was the true treasure. Captain Neville's presence in the forest, his attempts to set things right, revealed the truth to them."

Dorothy looked at Trafalgar. "She erased his memory so he wouldn't come after her again. If he remembers..."

"We will have to protect her, not only from the Burnt Empire but from Neville himself. Difficult to do if we're not in the same timeline."

"If we protect her from the Burnt Empire, perhaps... there may be an overlap..." She pressed her fingers to her temples. "Goddamn it, I hate this! We'll deal with Neville when and if he presents a threat. For now, we have to hope Cora realizes the threat he poses and stands in his way."

Snakes had started flowing into the room like an inky river. Black, orange, yellow, red, white, they all blended into a single sea of writhing scales. Dorothy tried to step back out of their way, but the snakes moved across her feet on their way to the water. She decided it was safest to remain still and let them go where they wanted to go.

"They only attack if provoked," Trafalgar said.

"That is not helpful."

Trafalgar said, "Just relax."

Dorothy took a steadying breath and remained motionless until the last tail had passed over her foot. The water seemed alive now, unsettlingly active just beneath the surface. D'janira stood and went to the edge of her platform. She crouched and slipped her hand into the water to allow one of the slender snakes to wrap around her wrist before continuing up her arm. She let it settle across her shoulders and smiled at its diamond-shaped head. Then she looked at Dorothy and Trafalgar.

"Let's begin."

CHAPTER SEVENTEEN

CORA AND Rute were preparing to descend into the caves when Ketcham called them over to Captain Neville. "I think he's beginning to come around."

Cora crouched beside the older man. "Felix? Can you hear me?" She pressed her hand to his forehead. His skin was red and warm. His eyelids fluttered and then opened, staring at her without focusing. She smiled and moved her palm to his cheek. "There you are, Captain. You gave us quite a fright."

"Lady Boone?" His voice was rough, raspy.

"No, it's me. It's Cora Hyde."

He squinted. The lines around his eyes seemed deeper. "I apologize. I don't believe we've had the pleasure. I'm Captain Felix Neville."

"I..." Cora glanced at Ketcham. "What do you remember, Captain?"

He searched the ground next to him. "Do I have a canteen? I need water." Rute stepped forward and offered hers. He thanked her and took a long drink from it. When he finished, he handed it back. "Dorothy Boone and I traveled from the... the wreckage of Flight 372. She was going to help me undo the damage I caused to history. We were traveling with... with..."

Ketcham said, "Rute and myself."

Neville looked at him, then at Rute. "No. I don't believe so."

Cora said, "How can he not remember either group?"

"He remembers Boone," Rute said.

"Well, Dorothy Boone is a bit unforgettable," Cora said. "But if anything, he should remember *all* of us. Arriving at this place seemed to merge the man from both timelines into one. Captain Neville, look at me. Do you remember Miss Trafalgar?"

"Yes," he said. "She was... with me, briefly... I think. We stayed at the camp for a while. She was hurt. She was ill..."

Cora nodded. "Yes, that's true. Someone came with her to the camp. Someone helped you carry her. Do you remember? You offered her coffee, but she asked for tea..."

"So civilized. A true British woman, after being so long among Americans and savages." There was a touch of a smile on his face. "A lovely woman. Black hair..." He looked at her, and she saw recognition in his eyes. "Was that you, my dear? I'm so sorry. It is my mind that's faulty. I'm certain a better man would find you impossible to forget."

She tried not to blush at the blatant flirtation. "It's quite all right. You've had a harrowing couple of months." She remembered the painkillers from Trafalgar's bag and motioned for Ketcham to hand it to her. "We have medicine that will help you handle any pain you're feeling. Mr. Ketcham will stay here in case you need anything."

"Where are you going to be?"

Cora nodded to the cave. "We have to find Miss Trafalgar and Lady Boone. They went into the cave yesterday and we haven't heard from them since."

Felix grabbed her wrist. She was too surprised to cry out, and his grip was too strong for her to pull free. She stared at him in surprise as he sat up straighter, the life returning to his face.

"You cannot go down there. I always intended to go down alone, with the rest of you safe up here." His second wind was fading fast. He was slumped over now, his hand merely resting on Cora's wrist. "She's too... she's dangerous..."

"Who?"

Felix closed his eyes. "The woman. She's the powerful one. I woke her up. I caused all of this to happen. I set it in motion and... it's my fault." He swallowed hard. "I can't remember... my mind... she did something to my mind..."

Rute cleared her throat. "Maybe I could try something."

Cora was hesitant, but she didn't feel they had many options available to them. She moved out of the way and let the larger woman kneel next to Felix.

"Captain Neville, do you remember me?"

"No. Seems to be going around." He looked at Ketcham. "You... are bland enough that I might not even remember you if I was healthy."

Ketcham twisted his lips, uncertain if he should waste the energy to be offended.

"My name is Rute. You may not know me, but I know you very well. We've spent a lot of time together over the past few weeks. I want you to close your eyes and remember a year ago. Before the Burnt Empire existed. You had just arrived in the forest. You had the location of the Pratear that someone had given you. It was written on a piece of paper and slipped under your hotel room door. It brought you here, to this spot. It told you to look for the cave. You climbed down. And once you were below the surface, what did you find?"

He looked like he was asleep, but his eyelids were parted just enough to see the whites through the lashes. "D'janira."

Cora looked at Rute, impressed.

"And who is she?"

"Not who." He was still speaking as if in a dream. "She's... something else. Something different. I woke her up. I thought she was... protecting the river. She wasn't. It's *her*. The river is just... where she... lives. She's the thing. She's... it's her."

Rute shook her head. "I don't understand what he's talking about. Did that help you at all?"

Ketcham collapsed face-first on the grass, arms slack with no attempt to break his fall. Cora grabbed for the gun at her hip as Rute immediately rose into a fighting position. Something sharp pierced Cora's throat, followed by a second impact on her right shoulder. Cora's legs wobbled underneath her, both fists raised but moving in circles rather than braced for a fight. Cora reached for her, but all the strength seemed to have gone out of her limbs. She fell like laundry cut from the line and blades of grass pressed sharply against her cheek.

She couldn't close her eyes, and summoning the ability to speak or move an arm was out of the question. Rute's lower body was just barely in her line of sight and it seemed she had been equally incapacitated. Someone stepped over Cora, followed by two more people moving in from the sides. The clearing was suddenly full of people. Their trousers were oddly modern, and they had fashioned strange shoes out of thick strips of leather held together by string.

One of the men crouched down and twisted his head to look into her eyes. He had a patchy beard and thick, curly blonde hair.

"Hi there," he said with an accent she could have sworn was American South. "My name is Travis Peterson."

Cora managed to blink one eye shut, but couldn't open it again.

"That's all right. There's gonna be plenty of time for talking when we get back to our camp." He looked past her and scanned the trees. "I know you've got more people around here. The redhead and the tall black lady. Are they around here? Or did they go wandering off for food or something? You can just nod, or... make a sound or... damn." He looked over his shoulder at the other members of his group. "I'm not getting anything out of this one. I think you hit her with too much."

"She got in the way of the dart I shot at this one. But I think he's so looped that he would've died if we did tranq him, so we got lucky there."

"Sure, sure," Travis Peterson said. "What about the others?"

"Big lady is still mostly conscious, but she's not answering. The guy is completely out."

Travis shook his head. "Two women and a pair of fellas who look like they've both got their brains squashed. I told you we shouldn't have used the darts."

"What do you want to do?" the other man asked. "We can wait and see if their friends come back."

"Nah, we've already lost most of the day. Have Jeremy stand watch. If the missing ladies show up, he can take care of them himself."

"What if they went into the caves?"

Travis said, "Then they've got bigger problems than we do. Come on, let's get them up and get moving. I bet these ladies aren't as light as they look."

He grabbed her around the waist and hauled her up with effort, grunting as he slung her over one knobby shoulder. Cora couldn't do anything but dangle and stare at his back as he started walking. She could only assume that Rute, Ketcham, and Felix were being treated to the same indignity by the other members of Travis' party. The sound of moving water faded as they were carried into the heavy foliage and she realized with dismay that, if they went far enough, they would never be able to find their way back to the cave or their camp.

There was little she could do about it now. Dorothy and Trafalgar were on their own, and she was now a prisoner of the Burnt Empire.

"What time is it?"

The question was so unexpected that, at first, Dorothy assumed she'd misheard. She put her hand against her hip where she usually kept a pocket watch. She looked at Trafalgar, who was equally at a loss. Their timepieces were back with the rest of their wet clothing. Being underground meant that she also couldn't use the quality of sunlight to make an educated guess.

"I'm not certain," Dorothy said. "I assume it's not long after dawn."

D'janira said, "The sun began brightening the sky about thirty minutes ago. Sixty seconds repeated thirty times. Meaningless to the sun and its actual progression across the sky. The day begins when it begins, and no amount of marking heartbeats will change that. It doesn't matter what time it is, to the exact minute, just as it doesn't matter what day of the week, or the month, or the year."

"You're beyond such matters?" Trafalgar said.

"Beyond, above, removed from... it's insignificant in the grand scheme of things. Time is simply perception. Humans perceive things happening in a single moment because it would drive them mad to see everything all at once. Your mission is to prevent an aircraft from entering an anomaly fifty years from now and being sent to a point hundreds of years in the past."

"That's correct," Dorothy said.

D'janira shook her head. "These things all occurred at the same time. They all happened right here, in this spot. You and Miss Trafalgar are experiencing this moment because you are in the same time stream. You were born to a moment and remained tied to it your entire lives because humans cannot cut that string. At least not yet. One day you will find the secret."

"So by that logic, we've always known it," Trafalgar said.

"Yes."

Dorothy said, "When we get home, I am destroying every damned clock I can find. This is driving me insane."

"Allow me to demonstrate."

D'janira lifted her right hand. The room shifted and Dorothy felt sick to her stomach, as if the ground was being tilted and spun at the same time. She reached out and grabbed Trafalgar's hand for balance only to find Trafalgar had been reaching for her as well. Dorothy closed her eyes and tried to find her equilibrium, swallowing her nausea and finally forcing her eyes open. Everything was the same as it had been a moment before, but there was an added element: she saw herself and another Trafalgar standing across the room.

Their duplicates were wearing the wet clothes Dorothy had last seen in the chamber where they spent the night. They were speaking to another version of D'janira. Dorothy remembered enough of the conversation to read her own lips. She wanted to move closer but feared breaking the spell. She thought back to that moment and tried to recall if she'd seen anything else in the cavern, any hint of a ghost from the future lurking in the background, but she couldn't say for sure.

"Of course we were all present for this, so it's not enlightening."

D'janira held up both hands palm-out and spread them apart as if opening a window. The day-old images of Dorothy and Trafalgar vanished to be replaced by someone new.

Captain Neville.

He looked younger and more polished than the man she'd last seen on the surface. His clothes were clean and unpatched, and his hair was cut close to his scalp. He was scanning the room with awe, and Dorothy realized he couldn't see them. Light from his torch reflected off the water and made the stone walls look alive with movement. Except... no. The walls *were* moving, covered with curtains of snakes. She couldn't tell if the snakes were 'now' or 'then,' but she chose to believe they were phantoms.

Neville moved closer to the edge of the water. He moved the light of his torch over the plinths before stretching out one leg to test its stability with the toe of his boot. He judged it safe and hopped onto it. They watched as he continued across the pool in this manner, testing a plinth before trusting it with his weight until he finally reached the center where D'janira was currently standing. She moved out of his way and Dorothy saw what appeared to be a stone well.

"That isn't here... or wasn't... it's..." She shook her head. "That's gone now, isn't it?"

"Yes."

Trafalgar sounded like she was on the verge of breaking down. Dorothy realized she was still gripping Trafalgar's wrist, so she moved her palm down and linked their fingers together. Trafalgar squeezed her hand in response.

Neville circled the well. In the light of his torch, Dorothy saw the well was closed off with a cover stone. He used his free hand to push it, then put down the torch and used both hands. His boots scraped on the ground and he bared his teeth. His grunting echoed off the walls. D'janira watched his efforts with detached interest, her hands behind her back and head tilted to the side. Her body was still wreathed by snaked like living jewelry.

"Blast." Neville ceased his efforts and straightened to stare at the well. He pulled a notebook from his back pocket and began scribbling. Eventually he sighed, closed the book, and returned it to his pocket. He circled the well, hands on his hips, examining the problem.

"This takes some time." D'janira lifted her hand again, and the scene shifted.

Neville now looked as if he had just finished a bare-knuckle bout. His jacket was discarded on the ground next to him, the collar of his shirt was open and darkened by sweat, and both sleeves were rolled up. He raised a shovel with both hands and brought the blade of it down on the stone. The stone had obviously already been weakened by a great many blows, and this was the one which caused the wooden handle of the shovel to splinter. Neville stumbled and stared at his now-useless tool.

"Blast!" His shout echoed off the water and rock. "Blast and damn and blast!" He threw both pieces of the shovel, now two spears, and dropped to his knees in defeat. "God damn it to hell..."

After a long, defeated moment, he lifted his head. He wiped his forearm across his face and, with great effort, got back to his feet. He walked to the well, looked at the cracked cover stone, and gave a startling, animalistic shout. He raised both fists over his head and brought them down with all the strength he still possessed.

The stone shattered.

He recoiled in shock and then continued his retreat when a knot of snakes began writhing out of the now-open well. Trafalgar pulled Dorothy a step backward at the sight of them. Neville shrieked and tried kicking at them, then ran to retrieve the discarded pieces of his shovel. The snakes swarmed him. They wrapped around his ankles and kept him from advancing. He fell forward, arms extended and stopping his fall while presenting his wrists to more of the serpents.

"This is it," Dorothy whispered. "This is the moment that led to the anomaly."

Trafalgar nodded but seemed unable to take her eyes off the scene playing out before them.

The past version of D'janira looked haggard and weak. She sat on the rim of the well and stared at the snakes before she noticed the man sprawled among them.

"You woke me."

"I... I was..." He groaned and tried pushing a snake away, but it coiled around his hand. "Call them off. Please, tell them to leave..."

"I don't control them." She slipped off the well. The snakes writhed around her feet but did nothing to impede her progress. "Did you come to free me, sir, or control me?"

Neville said, "I didn't... know you were here. If I had..."

D'janira's face darkened. It felt as if all the air was sucked from the room, and the snakes converged on Neville. He screamed and brought up his hands to prevent them from sliding into his mouth. D'janira moved to stand over him.

"If you did not come to free me, then you are here to exploit my gifts. You want to *steal* it."

The snakes were now around Neville's throat, tightening slowly.

"Please," he gasped. "Let me live and I will assist in your liberation."

"Lies."

His face was rapidly changing colors. He tried to get his fingers under the snakes, but their bodies were obviously too strong and their scales slick with water from the well.

"You wish to live?"

Neville could only make a grunting noise at this point, but Dorothy saw his chin lift and drop in a nod. The snakes responded to some invisible signal and loosened their grip on him. D'janira crouched at his feet and rested her elbows on her knees.

"The damage you've caused is already creating ripples. The echoes are forming even now." She looked directly at Dorothy and Trafalgar, holding the gaze of both women before moving on to look at other things that only she could see. "The damage you have caused will also be mended through your actions. You will bring others and they will heal the scar. But you must survive for that to happen."

"Thank you," Neville said. "I promise, I will bring them back. I'll~"

D'janira put her hand over his mouth. "You will not remember..."

The scene faded and Dorothy was suddenly lightheaded. She stumbled, nearly fell, and then choked back another wave of nausea.

"Are you well?" D'janira asked.

"I'll recover."

Dorothy looked at Trafalgar to make sure she was also recovering. She took a deep breath of cool air and stood up straighter. She faced D'janira.

"The Burnt Empire is on their way, aren't they?"

D'janira looked toward the ceiling of the cave as if she could hear footsteps on the surface above. "I do not know the hour of their arrival. But it approaches swiftly."

Trafalgar took a step closer to D'janira. "Tell us what we need to do."

CHAPTER EIGHTEEN

"LET ME tell you a story."

Cora was propped up against a tree not far from the Pratear and the cave where Dorothy and Trafalgar had vanished the day before. She still couldn't move but she could blink and breathe. Rute was lying flat on her back nearby, one hand on her stomach and the other sprawled out next to her. If it wasn't for her chest rising with the occasional shallow breath, she would look dead. Ketcham and Felix were sitting against trees directly across from Cora. Travis Peterson was standing between them, near Rute.

"It's a long story. It's the story of my ancestors. You see, one day a long time ago, they boarded an airplane in a place called Texas. During the flight, something happened. They never figured out what it was or where they went. A group set out to see what they could find, to learn where exactly they were, and they found civilization. Such as it was. That was when they discovered the horrible truth: they were hundreds of years in the past. They had no idea how that happened and definitely had no idea how to get home. All they knew was that they were trapped and had to survive somehow. So they got to work. They built homes. They planted food. And yes, in order to feed themselves and their families, sometimes they had to take from the people who were already here.

"I know what you're thinking. You're judging them. But imagine what those tribes would have thought! They either would have worshipped our ancestors as gods or burned them as demons. I don't know if they made the right choice. I don't know what I would have done in their position. But I know they were successful. They survived. They began to thrive in this inhospitable place. Babies were born. Soon this was their home."

He moved and bent at the waist to look at Rute. After a long moment where he seemingly assessed her health, he straightened and went to Ketcham.

"They kept a lot of things about their previous lives. Names. Language. Customs. They knew eventually time would catch up with us and someone would arrive to take us to the world we should have inherited. I think you're a little early, though. We've still got fifty years before the plane gets tossed back in time, if the calendars we've been using are right. But I think we can make it work. That's *my* opinion, of course. We'll see what our big boss man has to say when he gets here."

"Oh, I'm here."

Travis turned toward the brush from which the voice seemed to emanate, unable to hide his surprise. Another man appeared, a wry grin on his slender face.

"Jeremy," Travis said. "How long have you been there?"

"Not long. I just like hearing that story." Jeremy walked past Travis and examined the prisoners. "Well, who are these?"

Travis regained his focus. "Explorers. You know about Captain Neville, of course. These ones are new. That one," he pointed at Rute, "is a local. The others are British. There are at least two more, maybe three, who went underground."

Cora was surprised at the depth of his knowledge, spotty though it might have been, and wondered how long the Burnt Empire had been tracking them.

"Underground," Jeremy muttered. "Into the cave."

"Yeah. The very same."

Jeremy knelt down next to Cora and touched her cheek so they could look each other in the eye.

"What do you know, Miss London?" he asked. "What do your friends know? Can they reverse this?"

"Ahh~" Her tongue felt like stone in her mouth, but the ability to move her lips was an enormous relief. She blinked slowly. "Ahh."

Jeremy looked at her throat and twisted to look at Travis. "How much did you dose her with?"

"I may have gone a little overboard."

"Moderation, Mr. Peterson. We are working on a deadline, you know." He faced Cora again and sighed heavily. "Give me the stimulant."

Travis fumbled in his pocket and produced a small phial. Jeremy took it and twisted off the top. "My guys use this for themselves sometimes. They dip those darts they hit you with in it, prick their arms or necks or whatever, and it gives them a boost of energy. It makes the natives around here think we're superhuman or something. Are superheroes a thing yet...? I think it's a little too early for that. There were some comic books on our plane when it went down. Anyway, I don't really know how this will interact with the tranq, and you're going to get a much bigger dose than we usually give anyone. But we need to know what to expect in the cave. So bottom's up."

He held the phial against her lips and tilted it. Cora's mouth filled with a vile, nasty liquid that she had no choice but to swallow. Thankfully he didn't give her more than a mouthful, but it was enough that she nearly choked on it. She coughed and gagged, leaning forward. Jeremy put a hand on her shoulder and moved to one side just in case she did manage to vomit up the poison.

"There we are! What's your name, new friend?"

"Corahyde." She squeezed her eyes shut. "Mynameiscorahyde. Goodlord." She could feel the throbbing of her pulse in her extremities, but she could barely catch her breath. Colors were sharper and the light was so bright it hurt her eyes. A wave of shudders passed through her and she choked back a cry of fear. "Whatdidyougiveme?"

"Just woke you up a little, darling. Just take deep breaths."

She pushed him away and got to her feet in a burst of motion. Travis grabbed for her, but she grabbed two of his fingers and twisted them until he yelped. She didn't let go and spun, using him as a counterweight. She only released him when his trajectory would send him tumbling into Jeremy. She didn't wait to see them hit the ground. She ran, but someone grabbed her arm and jerked hard enough to knock her down.

"Her damned heart is going to explode!" Travis said. "Hold her down!"

More Burnt Empire men jumped on her. Cora punched, clawed, bit, and growled at them, but she couldn't fight them all off. Jeremy moved to where she could see him.

"Sorry about that. The drugs should balance each other out in time. For now, you should take the opportunity to answer my questions. How many people went into the cave?"

"Twenty hundred!" Cora snapped.

Jeremy rolled his eyes. "Miss... Hyde, was it? We're going after them regardless of what you tell us. We just want to know what sort of response we'll receive."

Cora started to tell him where he could stick his interrogation, but her mind was running as fast as her heart. She pulled feebly at her captors and then closed her eyes as if in defeat. She growled, feigning frustration.

"You have to promise you won't hurt them."

Jeremy said, "I could be persuaded to show mercy."

Cora pretended to consider her options. She tried to convey the weight of a difficult decision, and settled on a look between resignation and fear. She wet her lips, still breathing hard.

"Two. There are only two of them."

"Tell me their names."

"Dorothy and Trafalgar."

Travis said, "I assume Trafalgar is the African woman?"

Cora swallowed and nodded.

Jeremy looked skeptical. "Two women...? That's all?"

"They were small enough to fit through the crack," Cora said, "and light enough for me to act as a counterweight when lowering them down."

"Armed?"

Cora said, "They were exploring. They took their journals, but didn't think weapons would be necessary."

Jeremy laughed. "Two unarmed librarians. And to think I was worried." He nodded at Travis. "Go into the caves, find this... Dot and Trafalgar. Preserve our history by whatever means possible."

"You said you wouldn't hurt them!"

"I said I could be persuaded," Jeremy said. "I was unconvinced. Get her up, restrain her. Make sure the ropes are good and tight so she can't muscle her way out. That stimulant will run out eventually, but better safe than sorry."

Cora kicked and writhed to get away as she was dragged back to her tree. As they wrapped ropes around her midsection, she hoped her ruse had worked. If they knew what they were actually up against, they might show precaution. But if they thought Dorothy and Trafalgar were helpless and frail women, they wouldn't waste time with stealth. Hopefully that would be enough to warn them.

Travis and a group of other men headed off to follow their orders, while Jeremy supervised the bindings. The stimulant and tranquilizers seemed to be fighting a battle in her bloodstream. She felt lightheaded and dizzy. Her tongue felt sluggish but the words still wanted to rush out of her. She struggled to keep her eyes open and focused on the man standing in front of her.

"You have to understand," Jeremy said, "that this isn't malicious. You're the villains in our eyes. You're trying to wipe us from history. You want to erase our very existence. We're simply fighting for our lives."

"You've slaughtered countless people in the past hundred years. Those lives were not less important than your own. Your parents, your grandparents, *their* parents, none of them should ever have been in this forest to begin with. If you were meant to be born, then you were meant to be born hundreds of years in the future. Your life... your true life, the one you were meant to have before the anomaly was created, it must be magnificent. Don't you want to see it?"

"I can have a magnificent life right here. I can build it with my own two hands."

Cora sighed. She was exhausted but also couldn't stop her eyes and fingers from twitching.

"Damn it, you fool. We're trying to set things right."

Jeremy said, "That's the problem, Cora Hyde. Our idea of what's 'right' are mutually exclusive. We can't both be right. So I'm going to go ahead and bet on the one that keeps me breathing."

"For the time being," Cora muttered.

He laughed and gestured at the ropes. "Make sure those are nice and tight, fellas."

Cora closed her eyes and let her chin drop onto her chest. *Be safe*, she thought, hopefully sending positive energy to Dorothy and Trafalgar wherever they were.

D'janira could "see" there would be four Burnt Empire men coming into the caves. Dorothy went through her pack and found a pistol and a machete, and Trafalgar reported having similar. They laid their weapons out so she could inventory their ammunition. She was certain they would have enough to fend off four men, but how many more were waiting on the surface? Dorothy remembered the rifles Ketcham and Rute had been carrying and found herself wishing she'd appropriated one of them. She wondered what had become of the people they left on the surface and hoped Cora was unharmed.

"I don't suppose you'll be lending us any assistance," Dorothy said. "Your snakes would be a very nice asset to have in our corner."

"They are not weapons," D'janira said, "nor are they servants to be ordered around."

"Of course," Dorothy muttered. She straightened and looked toward the entrance to the cavern. "We do have the advantage of knowing where they'll be coming from. And they have to descend the wall before they have a chance to defend themselves."

Trafalgar said, "You're willing to shoot them in the backs?"

"Knowing with certainty that they would kill us given the opportunity? It's not ideal, but I'll do whatever I have to in order to protect us." She looked at Trafalgar. "What would you suggest?"

"An ambush. Further down the corridor, where they won't be expecting us."

Dorothy said, "We'd be sacrificing the upper hand."

"In exchange for the element of surprise."

"There's too much potential for it to go wrong. If they spot us, we'll be cornered with no route for escape or retreat." She looked at D'janira. "Would you care to weigh in? This is your life we're protecting, after all, and you can see everything that's going to happen."

"Telling you wouldn't change anything. Either you will do what I tell you, or you will attempt the other strategy to prove the future can be altered."

Dorothy growled and rolled her eyes. "This prophecy nonsense is maddening! The future can be foretold but there's no point because we have just enough free will to make the information dangerous." She looked at the ground and considered their options. She weighed the danger of letting the Burnt Empire get close to their goal against the ethical dilemma of shooting them as they descended the cliff.

"We can't afford to be completely moral in this case. We have to consider what they would do in our position, and they would definitely stop us when we were most vulnerable. We'll wait for them at the cliff and eliminate them as they descend."

Trafalgar pressed her lips together. "I suppose it doesn't make sense to take a vote since we'd cancel each other out."

Dorothy said, "I'm sorry. If we had more time, I would be happy to strategize with you until we agreed. We don't have that luxury, and the one person with the answers won't help us cut out the middleman. We need to get into position as soon as possible."

"Right."

Trafalgar stooped to retrieve her weapons and Dorothy did the same. D'janira had remained motionless during the exchange.

"Stay here," Dorothy said. "If you hear anyone but us coming back down that corridor, politely ask the snakes to squeeze them to death."

She followed Trafalgar into the darkness, rushing to keep up with her so she could use the light of Trafalgar's torch instead of drawing her own. Soon the light of D'janira's chamber faded and they were once again enclosed in stone and darkness.

"I suppose it's good to know last night's activities didn't change anything."

"I beg your pardon?" Dorothy said.

Trafalgar kept her eyes forward, the beam of her torch on the water. "You still insist upon having your own way. You call this a partnership and you follow through on that when it's convenient to you. But when the chips are down, you ignore anyone else's input."

Dorothy inhaled slowly, counting to ten before she spoke. "And you believed what we shared last night would have changed that?"

"I don't know what I expected," Trafalgar muttered angrily. "I don't *want* for anything to change, but I suppose I was hoping there might be some benefits to our newfound... to this... whatever it might be."

Dorothy stepped forward and put a hand on Trafalgar's shoulder. The taller woman was outlined with the torch's light and, when she turned around, it washed golden across one side of her face.

"Last night was about us. It wasn't about working together or being partners. It was about a woman I've come to know very well and respect even more. Everything we've been through together, the hells we've faced together, and we've never shared the most intimate and lovely moments. That is what it was. That's what it meant. As for the other thing... there's some truth in that, but I also hope it's a bit unfair. I want to hear your ideas. You're a brilliant woman and you did just fine at this sort of thing before I came along. If my actions led you to believe I don't respect your opinion, then I sincerely apologize. It's simply that right now, in this instance, we have very little time and I definitely believe we're making the right choice. Hopefully we'll have a chance to fully debate it on the trip home."

Trafalgar stared silently at her and then closed her eyes. "Crumbs..."

Dorothy raised an eyebrow, her lips twitching as she tried to suppress her smile. "I beg your pardon? That's my word."

"But it's applicable here." She sighed and hung her head. "I believe I may be at fault. I was offended you dismissed my idea. I was certain your reasons were personal. But the only thing personal was my reaction."

"It was a new experience for you," Dorothy said, her voice softer. "You're bound to have complicated feelings about it. This isn't the ideal place to deal with emotions like that."

"I apologize for snapping at you."

Dorothy shrugged. "You weren't entirely in the wrong. I have been a bit bull-headed in the past. Now that I'm aware of it, I'll strive to do better."

"Thank you."

She leaned in and pressed her lips to Dorothy's cheek and, after a moment, her mouth. Dorothy rested her hand on the lapel of Trafalgar's tunic before sliding up to her shoulder. After a moment of enjoying the kiss, Dorothy turned her head and kissed Trafalgar's glowing cheek.

"Something else better left until our trip home."

"Right," Trafalgar said quietly. "The mission."

"Mm."

They stepped apart and continued onward.

The sound of falling water in the antechamber was louder than Dorothy remembered. She looked back the way they'd come, feeling as if they had emerged from a wholly separate world. She almost expected to see a shimmering veil just behind her. All she saw was darkness, so she examined the cave again. It was shockingly tall, a cathedral of glistening rock and plummeting water. She could hardly believe she'd scaled this wall just a few short hours earlier. The thought of climbing *up* was even more unbelievable to her, and she almost dreaded the return trip.

"We should take up position here," she said, "at the mouth of the corridor. We'll be concealed by the shadows and we'll have a perfect line of sight to the cave mouth." She looked at Trafalgar. "If that's all right with you, of course."

"It's a solid plan."

"Thank you."

They pressed their backs against opposite walls - Dorothy to the left, Trafalgar on the right. They had barely enough time to settle in before they heard splashing from above. Dorothy pressed harder against the wall, the stone cutting into her shoulder as she eyed the cave mouth. She could see people on the other side as they approached the opening.

"We'll wait until they're at the base of the cliff," Dorothy said. "Our guns won't reach much further than that anyway."

Trafalgar nodded, the move almost hidden by the shadows she'd stepped into.

Someone crouched at the cave entrance. With the sun behind him, he was little more than a black silhouette. Dorothy watched his head swing one way, then the other, before he swung his arm in a gentle lobbing motion. A few seconds later she heard something hit the ground and begin rattling as it rolled away. She spotted the little black-green device just as it tapped against the wall and began rolling back toward the water.

"Damn it," Dorothy said, "retreat!"

Trafalgar had time to step into the center of the corridor and push Dorothy behind her. The grenade exploded with a strangely quiet 'pop' which echoed through the room, and Trafalgar jerked and grunted in Dorothy's ear.

"Are you hit?"

"Shrapnel." Trafalgar put her hands on Dorothy's shoulders. "Go!"

Dorothy grabbed Trafalgar's arm to help pull her along but another explosion sent a concussive wave down the corridor, knocking them off their feet again. When she put her hand on the ground to push herself up, something heavy and thick slithered across her fingers. She had dropped her torch and the beam hit the wall at an oblique angle to allow her to see that it was a snake. She looked up and saw the dark shape of D'janira coming toward them.

"Thank goodness," Dorothy said. "You decided to bring reinforcements after all."

"I'm afraid not, Dorothy Boone," D'janira said. "I knew that Captain Neville was not alone. If he simply vanished, more would come looking for him. I had to ensure that the mystery of his disappearance was not worth solving. Leaving the well exposed and creating the anomaly was not part of my plan, nor was the creation of the Burnt Empire. I had to wait until they arrived before I could act. But now I have you all here. I can protect the Pratear once and for all."

"People will come for us," Trafalgar said. Snakes had continued flowing over them, heavy enough to keep them from standing up.

D'janira shook her head. "I've seen how this unfolds. I assume whoever funded you will decide against risking a third expedition. The Pratear will remain a myth. I am deeply sorry it has to be this way, but you must imagine what this gift could do in the wrong hands."

A snake wrapped itself around Dorothy's neck. She grabbed at it, but another sank its fangs into her hand. She cried out and then regretted the waste of air as the serpent constricted and kept her from inhaling. She could feel them heavy and writhing on her back. She already couldn't feel her hand, the numbness now spreading past her wrist.

"You don't have to do this..."

"This is my duty," D'janira said. "I'm sorry it has to be this way."

Dorothy's arms couldn't hold her up anymore, so she dropped. The water of the Pratear lapped against her face as she heard the sound of men shouting and opening fire from the main chamber. It seemed as if the snakes had found the Burnt Empire.

"We can protect you." Trafalgar sounded as weak as Dorothy felt.

D'janira sounded almost kind when she said, "I wish you could understand. That is exactly what you are doing."

The last thing Dorothy heard was a single word whispered as D'janira rested a hand on top of her head.

"Goodbye."

CHAPTER NINETEEN

SOMETHING SHARP sank into Cora's thigh, just above her knee, and her attempt to cry out in shock and pain was stymied by a hand over her mouth. She stared unblinking at the person who had stabbed her, startled to see Rute's wide eyes behind a mask of mud, crushed leaves, and dried blood. Rute put a finger against her own lips and checked over both shoulders to make sure they were still alone.

"The stimulant wore off and you were unconscious again," Rute whispered. "I couldn't wait for you to wake up on your own. Do you think you can stand?"

Cora looked down at herself and discovered the ropes tying her to the tree had been severed. She nodded and accepted the hand Rute offered her.

"They all went to the lake. They left us behind because they assumed you were drugged, and that Ketcham and I were dead."

Ketcham was sprawled nearby. Only then did Cora notice half of his head was missing. She recoiled from his corpse and looked away. "Good lord!"

Rute grunted. "They made sure with him, but didn't bother with me. I'm not sure if I should be offended or not, since their chauvinism saved our lives. Do you have any weapons on you?"

"No." She looked to where she had last seen Captain Neville, but he was gone. "Did they take Felix with them?"

"Not that he'll be much help," Rute said. She knelt beside Ketcham and patted him down. "The man was basically a walking corpse by the time they finally revived him. He's not long for this world, I'll bet. Keep your voice down. They aren't far."

A small brown book was lying in the grass, and she stooped to pick it up. She flipped it open to a marked page and skimmed the sloppy handwriting. "*Found source of Pratear. Mysterious well on stone platform in the center of a sub'tnan pool. MAGNIFICENT. I can feel its power. I know it contains what I've come all this way to find. If I can only get inside, my treasure surely awaits!*" Those weren't the words of the man she had come to know. Granted, their friendship had been rushed, but surely she would have recognized this grasping opportunist. Regardless, she knew without a doubt who had written these words. Jeremy must have dropped it when she was first dosed with the stimulant.

"You can read later," Rute snapped.

"This is Captain Neville's journal! The Burnt Empire must have taken it when they attacked his expedition. Felix is the only one among us who actually went down into that cave and managed to come back again," Cora said. "I don't want to run in there blindly if we don't have to."

Rute considered that before she nodded. "Okay. That's fortunate."

She had found two knives and a revolver on Ketcham's body. She unfastened his ammunition belt and slung it over her shoulder. She rose into a crouch and craned her neck in an attempt to see Travis and his cronies through the trees. She crept closer to Cora and motioned for her to get down as well.

"There was an explosion not long before I woke you up," Rute said. "It came from underground. I felt it in my boots. Not long after that, I heard gunfire, also underground. Does that journal say anything helpful?"

Cora flipped back a few pages. "I'm making the assumption sub'tnan means subterranean, which means he found it after descending through the cave." She skimmed his scratched words. They knew about the cliff he would have had to climb because they'd sent Dorothy and Trafalgar down the same wall. Hopefully he would have been tired enough to stop and write an entry before he continued on.

"Here," she whispered, holding the book so Rute could see the page.

"I can't read English."

"Oh. My apologies. You, um, speak it very well." Rute ignored the awkward compliment. "He says the cliff leads to a wide area, and from there a corridor leads 'deeper into the earth.' He wrote that he could hear the sound of the river echoing off the walls." The handwriting was shaky here, either from excitement at being near his goal or his hands were weak from climbing down the wall."

Rute said, "One way in, one way out. It was an ambush for one or the other of them. I'm not confident about Trafalgar and Boone's chances. They went down with pistols, the Burnt Empire had rifles. Longer range."

"But the Burnt Empire would have to descend with their backs to the cave," Cora said. Almost immediately, she realized their plan. "The grenade would have sent Dorothy and Trafalgar running. If it didn't kill them right away. We can only hope they were deeper in the cave when it went off." She looked at the weapons Rute had gathered. "I can handle a gun if that's what you're wondering. I have no problem shooting these bastards in the back if we need to."

Rute shook her head. "We're not shooting anyone if we don't have to. Come on." She turned and headed back the way they'd come the day before.

"Excuse me?" Cora said, remaining where she was.

"Going to the cave is a suicide mission, Miss Hyde. Your friends are dead. Captain Neville is dead. I'm not going to throw my corpse on top of theirs. We're going to use these weapons to get back to camp, recover whatever we can, and then I'm taking you back to Belém. I imagine this place will always be part of your nightmares, unfortunately, but physically... we're leaving it. Right now."

Cora's face burned. "No. Not again. Not this time, not with Dorothy and Trafalgar."

Rute furrowed her brow. "What are you talking about?"

Cora struggled to keep her voice low, but it had become a growl. "I will not run away. I will not spend the rest of my life wondering what happened, going over it in my mind, wondering if I could have saved them. No. I refuse. I refuse to leave their story unfinished." She stalked forward and held out her hand. "If you insist on leaving, then go. I'll take out every last fucking one of these bastards by myself if I have to."

"You will find only corpses!"

"Then I will bring their bodies home for a proper burial."

Rute said, "You're willing to die for this principle?"

"I couldn't bear living knowing I walked away again."

Rute squared her shoulders and held out one of the guns butt-first. "Congratulations, Cora Hyde. I think it's completely insane what you're doing, and I still think the only wise choice is to cut our losses, but if pushed, I'd say this is the moral choice. You're the first person in this entire damned expedition I actually respect."

Cora took the gun. "Then let's go. Time's wasting."

Gunfire. Dorothy's consciousness rushed back to her like a wave, like a sudden explosion of light in a dark room. She was sitting against something stone, her legs out in front of her. She couldn't feel either arm below the shoulders. She looked down and saw both hands resting on her lap like swollen bags of water. She could see where the snakes had bitten her, the twin hills radiating dark red trails up her forearms. Not good.

Also not good, the strobing light of continued gunfire which had brought her back to consciousness. She could see she'd been moved back into the main chamber, D'janira's inner sanctum. She realized she was in the center of the pool, which meant she was leaning against the broken well.

Trafalgar was lying facedown on the ground next to her. Her tunic was horribly ripped, the skin underneath torn and bloody. Dorothy saw chips of stone and pieces of metal shrapnel in the wounds and felt her rage building. Unfortunately her legs were as immovable as her arms.

D'janira stood guard at the edge of the water with her back to them, watching as the four unfamiliar men - presumably the Burnt Empire - used rifles to shoot at the snakes swarming around their feet. There were so many of them that it was impossible to see the stone beneath them. One man had two snakes hanging from either leg, hanging by the fangs embedded in his muscle. He tried kicking them away, but they only slapped against his calves like ribbons.

"Trafalgar... are you conscious?" Speaking was difficult and hurt her throat. If Trafalgar responded, Dorothy couldn't hear it. "I don't know how we're going to get out of this. You've always said I'm good at flying by the seat of my pants, but right now I think I'd prefer one of your carefully thought-out plans. Not that anyone could possibly have imagined us ending up in this predicament right now. So if you have anything, now would be the time to implement it. I'll follow along with whatever it is. Just take the lead and I'll... I'll follow..."

D'janira didn't turn around, but calmly said, "You've lived a taxing life, Dorothy Boone. You should accept your fate and enjoy the brief moments of peace you've been given. You've earned rest."

Every instinct told Dorothy to fight, but peace did sound so... appealing. And it wasn't as if she had many options. She couldn't lift her arms or stand. She thought she might be able to flop around like a beached fish, but that would be the extent of it. She would hardly be a force to be reckoned with. Maybe this really should be the end. It would be so easy to just surrender.

Two of the Burnt Empire men had fallen. One of them aimed his gun at D'janira, obviously hoping he could at least take her down with him, but the snakes took that chance to attack him en masse. He cried out in pain and terror and the shot went wide. D'janira didn't even flinch.

"You knew he would miss before he even pulled the trigger," Dorothy said. It was amazing how much effort it took to raise her voice to a casual speaking volume.

"Of course," D'janira said. "This has always been happening here."

Dorothy rested her head against the well. Fighting seemed even more pointless now. Another Empire tribesman fell, and now there was only one. He pulled off his belt, reached into a pouch, and with a battle cry which echoed off every wall and flat surface, flung it as hard as he could into the chamber. Dorothy watched it because her head was aimed in that direction, and it allowed her to see something unexpected.

D'janira flinched.

The belt flew across the room, farther and faster than it had any right to. It rose in a graceful arc and then began a slow descent toward the well. D'janira was following its progress as well, brow furrowed and lips parted. Dorothy felt a surge of hope at the realization the woman who could see everything - past, present, future - was *surprised.*

The belt hit the edge of the well and landed at the ground next to Trafalgar's outstretched right hand. The top flap had fallen open and Dorothy saw what was inside.

"Good lord. Trafalgar! Grenades!"

Trafalgar's hand moved slower than Dorothy would have hoped. She pushed herself up and, with what looked like herculean effort, grabbed the strap. Her face was twisted in a mask of agony as she lifted the bag and dropped it over the lip of the well.

"No! What are you... what have you done?" D'janira said.

The explosion threw Dorothy and Trafalgar away from the well. Its stone bulged outward, and she could hear something crackle deep beneath the surface. Dorothy felt fresh blood trickling down her forehead and wondered just how scarred she would be by this mission.

Not at all, she realized. *Scars need time to form...*

She rolled onto her back and looked at the well. White light shone from within, a beam of radiance unlike anything she had ever seen. It was magnificent until she realized the significance of what she was seeing.

"Oh, crumbs. We just created the anomaly."

D'janira was sobbing. "Why didn't I see this? I could have... stopped it. I could have saved us all." She fell to her knees and stared at the light.

Trafalgar was lying on her side, also staring at the light. One eye was swollen shut, and blood soaked the entire front of her tunic. Tears burned Dorothy's eyes. The expedition was worse than pointless, they had caused the very thing they intended to stop. She heard running footsteps coming up from behind her and twisted to see Felix Neville jumping from one plinth to the next, with Cora Hyde following closely. Cora froze when she saw the state Dorothy and Trafalgar were in, looking between them with no idea which one she should run to.

Felix, however, pushed D'janira out of the way to stare at the light. Unlike everyone else in the room, he seemed in awe of what he was seeing.

"At last." He held his arms out to either side, and Dorothy saw that he was holding his journal in one hand. "I've spent so long waiting for this moment. And now I'm here. I'm finally here. Everything I've worked for. But there's no sense in wasting time if I don't have to..." He smiled, laughed, and opened the journal to a blank page. He patted his pockets for a pen.

As Dorothy watched, she put several facts together in rapid succession.

Fact the first: They knew the anomaly could send things into the past.

Fact the second: Neville only found the cavern because he received a mysterious message on a trip to Brazil which gave him the coordinates.

Fact the third: They were only in this place because of Felix Neville's pursuit of the Pratear.

Fact the fourth: She had literally nothing to lose at this point.

She rolled onto her knees and threw herself at Neville like a sack of potatoes. She slammed into his lower body and knocked him to the ground. He cried out more from surprise than pain and twisted to look down at her.

"Lady Boone? Have you lost your mind? Get off of me this instant!"

"I'm afraid I can't do that, Captain Neville."

His expression changed. He gripped his pen tightly and lifted his arm above his head, then pistoned it down into her shoulder. The venom had numbed her enough that the wound didn't hurt nearly as much as it could have and, in fact, it provided enough adrenaline that she could bring her hands up to close them around his throat. She moved her body like an inchworm in the hopes her weight could pin him down, but she would lose any fight he would put up. Her death was an absolute given.

Or at least it was, until Trafalgar added her weight to the pile. She put her hands on top of Dorothy's and, though they were slick with blood, they were infinitely stronger than Dorothy's own grip. Neville choked and closed as she squeezed.

"What are we doing?" Trafalgar asked.

"Note. Neville sent... himself... coordinates. If we... he can't... we'll..."

D'janira said, "What are you trying to say?"

Dorothy looked back at her. "We have to close the loop. We've seen... alternate timelines. We know they can be created. We can create one by... preventing this man from sending himself a message. He'll never find this cave and this moment will never happen. None of us will ever come here." There was blood in her mouth, thick and metallic. "None of it will happen. The anomaly, the crash, the Burnt Empire. This will erase all of it. But this timeline has to be severed completely."

"Myself included," D'janira said.

"I'm sorry." She looked at Cora. "You should go. Leave. I don't know what's going to happen, but this cavern exists in an unusual pocket of time. Dying here may be permanent no matter what the timelines do."

Cora was crying. "I can't..."

"You can. You must. And help Trafalgar. She can still walk a little..."

Trafalgar said, "I won't leave you to die alone."

Dorothy met Trafalgar's gaze.

"Besides," Cora said, intruding on their moment, "time is of the essence, and there's no chance we could scale that cliff back to the surface anyway. We're doomed no matter what. We might as well make a united stand."

"Fine. I suppose it's too much to ask that my dying wish be honored." She looked at D'janira again. "Is there a way to ensure the complete destruction of this place?"

D'janira nodded. "Of course. If what you claim is true, it will continue in another timeline. I will live. But this version of me... will not. That is a difficult truth to accept."

"Trust me, I understand." Feeling was returning to Dorothy's torso and, judging from the pain that came with renewed sensation, she feared her death was imminent no matter what happened in the next few seconds. "But I believe it's the only way to end this once and for all."

"And I believe you are right."

D'janira faced the ruined well. She brought both hands up and the entire world seemed to shake around them. Dorothy tried to imagine what had happened in the other timelines. She and Trafalgar most likely died. Felix would have gone into the past to send himself the message. D'janira may have spent the next fifty years trying to rein in the anomaly only to fail in the end. The plane would be sent into the past, crash. And around it would go...

But not this time.

A massive diamond-shaped object rose from the water on the far side of the well. It seemed too large to fit in the cave with them, but it continued to rise. It tilted down and Dorothy saw the serpent's face. Each eye was the size of an airship's tire. It stared down at them with an intensity that showed Dorothy precisely why cultures might have worshipped something like this. Its tongue flicked out and Dorothy flinched. Trafalgar even brought up her hand as if to ward it off. Cora retreated to the edge of the stone platform, clearly regretting her decision to remain.

Only D'janira was unaffected by its arrival. "The time has come."

The serpent seemed to look directly at her.

"Yes." D'janira's eyes were wet with tears. "It's the only way."

The ground shook again. The cave began to crumble, the roof collapsing in small pebbles that soon became large stones. Cora covered her head and dropped into a crouch.

Dorothy looked at Trafalgar, who smiled at her.

It was the last thing Dorothy saw before a stone hit her in the temple with enough force to crack her skull.

CHAPTER TWENTY

DOROTHY WOKE in a wave of agony that faded completely before she could cry out. Her skull was broken. She reached up to touch her temple, only then realizing she could move her arms. The poison was... no. There was no poison. And her skull hadn't been broken by a falling stone. She was in a bed. An unfamiliar bed, but it was definitely better than a stone platform in an underground cave. She took a moment to explore the places where she expected to find damage only to touch smooth, unbroken skin.

She sat up slowly, distrustful of the comfort she found herself in. Light streamed through cream-colored curtains, turning the entire room golden. A book was lying on the bed next to her and she checked the title. It was a novel she'd actually been meaning to read for weeks, but she hadn't found the time. She opened it to the marked page and realized she did remember the storyline. She remembered reading it the night before when she got into bed. But no... she'd spent the night before with Trafalgar...

That memory prompted her to drop the book and throw back the blankets. She pulled open the door to a hotel corridor, posh and late-morning silent. Trafalgar was at the other end of the hall in loose pants and a sleepshirt looking as confused as Dorothy felt. She looked up and their eyes met, and Dorothy saw a look of such relief and joy that it made her laugh.

"You're alive." Trafalgar moved slowly as if afraid to break the mirage.

"And you're in one piece," Dorothy said. "I don't think you know just how much blood you were losing."

Trafalgar lightly touched Dorothy's face. "So it was real? The cave, the serpent... I saw you die.”

“You weren’t far from death yourself.” Dorothy put her hands on Trafalgar’s shoulders, grateful to feel how solid she was. “Cora?”

“I haven’t seen her.” Trafalgar looked over her shoulder, but the hallway was still empty. “Maybe she’s... no. No, she’s not here. She didn’t come with us.”

Dorothy could very clearly see Cora sitting across from her on the deck of the ship which brought them to Brazil. But she could also see the same tableau without her. She and Cora both applauded Trafalgar’s baldness, but she was also alone in her praise. They’d been a trio walking off the ship but also two women walking side by side.

“Who knows how much has changed,” she said. “For instance... last night...”

“Yes. Yes, last night. I remember it very well.”

Dorothy smiled. “Good. I would hate to think I’d only imagined it. But was it...”

“It was there,” Trafalgar said. “It didn’t happen here. We didn’t have the same experiences or near-losses to inspire the moment.”

“A shame.” She looked past Trafalgar and her confusion returned. “Where *are* we?”

“One of the nicer hotels Belém has to offer,” Trafalgar said. “You said since the RGS was footing the bill for this expedition, there was no reason we shouldn’t treat ourselves.”

“Right.” She now remembered saying those things. They’d been sitting in a bar, nursing some kind of fruity drink. “Please, come in.”

They went into Dorothy’s hotel room and she closed the door. “I have memories of being here, relaxing and enjoying the warm weather. But I also remember the humidity of the forest, sleeping rough. My hands...” She held them out in front of her and stared at the fingers, which were now unblemished. “I scaled a cliff.”

Trafalgar walked to the bed and sat on the edge of the mattress. “Just as I know I spent a day tracking through the forest with Felix Neville. You also experienced the same day, with the same man, but it was a completely different experience. Two separate timelines.”

“So which one is this?”

“Neither,” Trafalgar said. “This is a timeline created because we never went into the forest in search of Captain Neville because...” She trailed off and gestured for Dorothy to recall on her own.

The memory arrived without needing to search for it. “We weren’t sent to *find* Captain Neville at all. We knew exactly where he was when we left London.” She could almost hear the voice of Bertram Rees as he addressed the Society members. “He was hunkered down on his ship. He would occasionally venture out to chase one theory or another, but always returned empty-handed. The members of his expedition abandoned him. One at a time, but then later in droves."

Trafalgar said, "We weren't sent to find him at all. We were sent to convince him to abandon his fool's errand. Mr. Rees hoped to get his ship back along with whatever supplies Neville hadn't yet burnt through. I don't understand why we're here now, though. What changed?"

"Neville received a mysterious note telling him where to find the Pratear. He was in front of the well when the anomaly was created. I believe he was the one who sent the note to himself. I stopped him. So he never found the Pratear, we never followed him there, the anomaly never opened. No airplane crash. No Burnt Empire."

Trafalgar took a moment to process that. "But his obsession remains."

"Apparently." Dorothy chewed her bottom lip. "If we remember both timelines, then surely he must as well. He'll know how to find the Pratear and everything we did will be rendered moot!"

"I survived longer than you did," Trafalgar said. "D'janira stepped forward and embraced him. The..." She looked away and, for a moment, Dorothy would have sworn she was about to say 'god.' "The serpent descended on them both. I don't know what it meant, but I have a feeling Captain Neville didn't arrive in this timeline quite as intact as us."

Dorothy joined Trafalgar on the bed. "You... survived longer than I did. That means you saw my death."

Trafalgar didn't turn to look at her. "It was devastating... A stone hit your head. It was clear that you were... The state you were in, I knew there was no..."

"Trafalgar."

Dorothy leaned in and touched her cheek, then replaced her fingers with her lips. Trafalgar turned her head and they kissed. It felt like their first, though Dorothy knew how Trafalgar would taste, would feel against her, and she knew the weight of Trafalgar's body on top of hers. When she pulled back, she knew that Trafalgar would lean in just a little as a sign of how much she wanted to continue. She moved her hand to Trafalgar's jaw and used her thumb to brush across her mouth.

"I'm so sorry you had to see that. And I'm shamefully grateful that I was spared the sight of your death." Her eyes stung with tears. "With all the awful things I've been witness to, that is one I don't believe I could bear. And I fear we risk losing something very precious if we don't act quickly. We don't know if our memories of what happened in the other timeline will linger, or for how long. At the moment, I know that you and I have made love. I recall it very vividly."

"As do I."

"But as the day wears on, there's a chance we might... lose those memories." She leaned closer. "I would not want for that to happen."

"Nor would I," Trafalgar said, closing the distance to kiss Dorothy's lips.

Dorothy grabbed a handful of Trafalgar's sleepshirt and lowered herself to the mattress without breaking the kiss, smiling as Trafalgar willingly settled on top of her.

"Just for my own accounting," Trafalgar said, "will this be our first encounter or our second?"

"Oh, Trafalgar, is the memory of last night already fading?" She kissed Trafalgar's neck, her hands roaming underneath the soft cotton to find warm skin. "This will be our fourth."

Trafalgar laughed and began pulling at Dorothy's clothes.

Cora opened her eyes and stared at the wall of her library. Outside, London rain pattered against the windowpane. She was at home. She was in her comfortable clothes just after a bath. But a moment ago...

A moment ago, she had been somewhere else. She had been... dying. She put down the book in her hands and placed one palm flat against the bookshelf. She closed her eyes and saw a cave entrance, and she knew that her friends had gone into that darkness without her. Tears broke free from her eyes and rolled down her cheeks. Her breath was difficult to catch as she saw the cliff face in front of her. She'd gone after them. She had gone into that pit and found Dorothy and Trafalgar.

"I didn't leave them behind," she whispered. "I found them. I may not have saved them, but I fucking went after them."

She stepped back until she felt the wall against her shoulders. She either sobbed or laughed, either way releasing a new wave of tears as she slid down and sat on the floor. She didn't know what had happened, not exactly. She knew there were timelines and consequences and new histories, and apparently now she was in a version of the world where she hadn't accompanied Dorothy and Trafalgar on their mission. But she had definitely been in Brazil. She'd been given a chance to redeem herself, to live down her cowardice, and she'd succeeded. For the first time since losing those poor girls, she felt free to breathe.

"Thank you, ladies," she said, aiming her words at the window. "Wherever you may be right now, thank you. God, thank you so much..."

She wrapped her arms around herself and sobbed, laughed, and let herself get used to the feeling of being released from her self-made prison. She didn't know when she would go on another mission, but she knew for a fact she was ready.

Whatever the world might throw at her, she was ready for it.

"I believe the memories are already fading," Trafalgar said, breathless, sweaty. "I don't remember it being anything like that."

"In a good way...?"

"In a fantastic way."

Dorothy giggled playfully and let her arms fall to her sides. "Never underestimate the value of a proper bed when it comes to lovemaking."

Trafalgar lifted one foot and wrapped her toes around a bar of the headboard. "Yes, you utilized this quite well, I must say."

"Why, thank you."

They were lying together like puzzle pieces, Trafalgar's head on Dorothy's shoulder. Dorothy's legs were mostly off the bed, but Trafalgar believed her feet were dangling a bit. She was a bit cramped in her position, her knees bent so she could fit on the bed. They stared at the ceiling for a moment before Dorothy gave a weary sigh and sat up. She scooted to the edge of the bed and got up, pausing to work out a kink in her back before she walked to the armoire in the corner. Trafalgar rolled onto her side and appreciated the curve of Dorothy's back, the span of her hips, and the muscles of her legs.

"You told me we were more than the sum of our scars. I think that's true, but I also think we are nothing but scars. Some good, some bad, but they all combine to make us the person we end up being. We're wounded. We heal. We change. Everything we did over the past few days... it still happened. It's still a part of us, even if they don't leave lasting marks."

Dorothy paused and considered that. "I can subscribe to that." She put on her underwear and began searching for a blouse.

"Where are we going?"

"We have to meet with Captain Neville. I know we've spoken with him several times on this trip, but we have to convince him to turn back. We have to bring him home or else he might get lucky and this whole blasted cycle will begin again."

Trafalgar said, "Maybe it won't. Maybe we delayed the birth of the anomaly long enough that the airplane won't pass through it."

"But who knows what other catastrophe might be caused? We have to convince him the search isn't worth his effort." Dorothy looked back at the bed and slowly let her eyes travel the length of Trafalgar's body. After the first initial feeling of shyness, Trafalgar lifted her chin and accepted the examination. She was pleased to see a bright pink hue rising in Dorothy's ears. "Not that I'm complaining about the view, but you might want to get dressed as well."

"Perhaps I would be more persuasive to Captain Neville like this." She lifted her arm above her head and arched her back. "What do you think?"

Dorothy grinned. "I believe you would cause a ruckus getting to the docks like that. Go on, get dressed. We have our entire trip back to London to be decadent layabouts."

Trafalgar forced herself into a sitting position and searched for her discarded sleepshirt. "I look forward to that. And... what happens when we get home? When we're living under the same roof on Threadneedle Street? I know you and Beatrice have a unique arrangement but, as far as I know, she's never had to deal with you bringing one of your conquests home when the mission was over."

"No," Dorothy confessed. She looked down at the slacks she was holding. "I don't know what's going to happen when we get home, Trafalgar. I truly don't. What you and I shared here is more than some tryst. You aren't a conquest and this isn't something we'll just move on from. At least I hope it isn't." She finally looked up. "If you decide you don't... that is to say, if you decide you prefer to be with men. I won't take it personally."

"I don't know yet. Making love to you was magnificent." She lost her breath on that last word, and it took her a moment to continue. "But at the same time, I don't know if I've discovered something fundamental about myself or if I've simply learned something about how deep our relationship truly goes. I wouldn't feel right usurping what you have with Beatrice for something I can't even put into words."

Dorothy returned to the bed and cupped Trafalgar's face to make her look up. "I know Beatrice is an understanding woman. She isn't jealous, nor petty. To be honest, I'm not certain how I feel about this new tangle, either. It could be something beautiful. It could be a brief, wonderful distraction. We'll take our time to truly explore it before we make any rash decisions."

"Kiss me."

"Yes, Miss Trafalgar." Dorothy bent down and kissed Trafalgar's lips. "Mm. Whatever happens, I do hope those continue."

"I think I'd find it difficult to stop."

Dorothy brushed her thumb over Dorothy's cheek. "Good. Now go... get dressed. I'm famished, and I want to speak with Neville as soon as possible."

"Yes, Lady Boone."

Trafalgar finished dressing and slipped out of Dorothy's room. She realized as she crossed to her own room that she had no idea what time it was, and only a vague inkling of the day. She knew that, if asked, she would immediately say she'd spent the day before in the rain forest and then exploring a subterranean cave. But then she would correct herself. "Wait, no... no, that's ridiculous. I spent the day sightseeing here in town, since the man we came here to speak to has proven quite stubborn." She knew both things were true, but her mind rebelled at any attempt to reconcile the memories.

She also knew they had come to Brazil with Cora Hyde, but now she distinctly remembered being alone with Dorothy for the entire trip. She went into her room and looked at the bed. *I slept here last night,* she thought, even as her mind conjured images of lying naked on top of a stone bed with Dorothy Boone. She put a finger to her temple and shook her head.

In her time, she'd seen a great many strange and inexplicable things. This would just be one more piece of strangeness added to the pile. But she feared the memories would fade, that soon their time in the jungle and D'janira's cave would be little more than a dream. It would be best to transcribe it immediately before she lost any of the details.

There were notebooks in her bag and she retrieved one, settling at the desk in front of the window as she debated where to begin.

We engaged a tour guide by the name of Marco Eiriz to take us into the forest. This was the same man who had taken Felix Neville into the wilderness and claimed he could take us to the grave of our missing colleague...

CHAPTER TWENTY-ONE

DOROTHY REMEMBERED two versions of the same event, and she parried against both on their way to the harbor. In one scenario, Bertram Rees was composed but concerned. He feared Neville was dead and simply wanted that fact confirmed so the RGS could close their books on the matter. In the other scenario, Rees was equally composed but irritation was the emotion he tried to conceal. He and the RGS knew Neville was alive, but the captain refused to respond to their correspondence. Rees hoped the Mnemosyne Society could appeal to him as colleagues and convince him to come home. The others balked at what amounted to a babysitting session but Dorothy, as de facto leader of the group, saw it as her duty to help out. Trafalgar agreed to keep her company. Everything else played out the same in both memories, and she was flustered by the overlap.

When they arrived at Neville's ship, the *Herald*, Dorothy paused to consider the etiquette for boarding a ship without invitation. Trafalgar had no such qualms and continued up the gangplank with no hesitation. Dorothy decided she might as well follow.

The deck was littered with the debris of a man who had been living alone for too long: dirty plates, piles of discarded clothing, and other items put out in the fresh air so they wouldn't sully his living quarters. The ship was silent save for the groan of wood and rigging. Dorothy examined everything as if she was seeing it for the first time, but she also remembered being in this very place the day before, and the day before that. She shook her head and hoped the strange duality of her memories would settle with time.

"Captain Neville?"

Something clattered in one of the interior rooms. Dorothy and Trafalgar went toward the noise and found Captain Neville on the bridge of the ship. He was unshaven, his hair long but mostly tamed in a ponytail. He was wearing a filthy shirt unbuttoned over an unwashed chest, and Dorothy grimaced at the sight of him. It was a far cry from the man she'd met in the airplane's wreckage. The floor was almost covered with defaced maps, shredded pieces of paper, discarded journals, and bottles which were mostly empty, though some were still dripping into the garbage pile. He seemed to be trying to tidy up the area.

"Save your breath, ladies," he said. "I'm sure you've come up with a very convincing argument but I don't need to hear it."

"Actually," Dorothy said, "we were just planning to wing it."

Neville gave her a distracted smile as he continued cleaning. "As I said, there's no need to waste your time. I've decided to go home."

Trafalgar said, "Really? Why the sudden change of heart?"

He paused and looked out the window, squinting in the sun. "I suppose your previous attempts burrowed their way into my brain, despite my best efforts to drink them away. I woke with a splitting headache, hungover, and nauseated. Some of that may be caused by sleeping on this blasted boat." He grimaced at the controls as if only just now noticing them. He turned away to face his guests. "I had a nightmare. Probably the most vivid, most harrowing nightmare I've ever experienced."

Dorothy feigned curiosity. "Do tell."

Neville stared at a spot on the wall. "It was a swarm of unconnected images. I saw myself in the jungle. There was a massive construction looming out of the trees. Some sort of vehicle, the likes of which I've never seen. I saw myself descending into a cavern, and a magnificent room with a pool and, in the center of the pool, a well. There was a woman. And, at the very end, a snake larger than any creature you can ever imagine. It was immense." He held his hands out in front of his face as if trying to shape the image from his dream out of thin air. "It was a beast."

"Sounds frightening," Trafalgar said.

"I feel as you must have felt when facing the Minotaur. Awe, tinged with terror. And I knew that this creature, this god, was the true source of the Pratear. It was what I had been searching for all these years. I saw myself standing in front of it at last."

Dorothy said, "And this is what convinced you to walk away once and for all?"

Neville focused on her again. "It wasn't the only thing I saw, Lady Boone. I saw you. And you, Miss Trafalgar. And others, people I don't recognize but who felt important to me. You were all dead. Your head was crushed by a rock, Dorothy. Trafalgar's back was ripped to shreds and her clothing was soaked through with so much blood I thought it was printed silk. I saw only death and destruction in my wake."

"That's awful," Dorothy said.

He rubbed his face. "I took it as an omen. I might eventually achieve my goal, but it would be terrifying in ways I couldn't even imagine. I've never liked snakes..." His voice trailed off and they gave him a moment to compose himself. "I realized you and Trafalgar and the unknown people were stand-ins for precious things in my life. The things I was destroying on this foolhardy quest."

Dorothy said, "That seems like a reasonable interpretation."

Neville gave a barking laugh and shook his head. "To be honest, the dream came too late to save me. My savings are gone. No one will ever crew with me again after this. Several of them swore that to my face before they finally abandoned me. As for the Royal Geographical Society, there is no chance they'll ever fund a future expedition."

"I'm sure that's not true..." Trafalgar said.

"Oh, of course it's true! They had to send you to come fetch me like I'm a disobedient child. My career is effectively over. The only thing that might have saved me is finding the Pratear. But that dream..." He trailed off again and looked out the window. "It felt as if I was living it. As if I was actually there. I felt the elation, the pride of knowing I'd finally succeeded. But I was covered with blood. I was soaked in it, and there were bodies piled at my feet. The cost is already much too high."

Dorothy nodded solemnly. "I'm sorry it has to end this way, Captain Neville. But you should know that if the RGS turns its back on you, there are others like us who know this type of obsession all too well. Your only sin was trusting your instincts. We've all been guilty of that while in the field."

"Some more than others," Trafalgar said.

Dorothy glared playfully at her. "The Mnemosyne Society won't turn its back on you. Whatever help you may require in the future, you can count on us to provide it."

"Thank you, Lady Boone, and Miss Trafalgar. I know it would have been easier to just lock me in the hold and commandeer my ship. I'm grateful you let me come to this conclusion on my own."

Trafalgar said, "If we'd forced you to leave, you would have just come running back at the earliest opportunity. At least that's what I would do."

Dorothy said, "As would I."

"I still have some work to do before this vessel is seaworthy. I'm willing to let the two of you ride along with me just to ensure this isn't a ruse and I don't turn around in the middle of the Atlantic."

"That won't be necessary," Dorothy said. "If you don't show up in London in an expedient manner, we'll just send a few of our meaner members to fetch you."

Neville managed to smile. "We wouldn't want that now, would we?" He stood and extended a hand to Dorothy. "Thank you."

"You have nothing to thank us for, Captain."

They both shook his hand, then left him to continue preparing for his voyage. Trafalgar waited until they were back on solid ground before she looked back at the ship.

"Do you believe he's truly seen the light?"

"I do. That haunted stare... I saw the same thing in Cora's eyes when she institutionalized herself. I would never wish that sort of pain or anguish on anyone, but I think he'll get through it since there are no actual corpses in conscience. He may be right about his future in our profession. We can invite him into the Society, but he may not be accepted by the other members. I can't imagine anyone else working with him after this debacle. Even if they knew the details of every timeline, the simple fact is that he went rogue."

Trafalgar said, "Pity. From all accounts he seemed like a good explorer."

"Mm." Dorothy slipped her arm around Trafalgar's. Trafalgar looked down but said nothing. "Speaking of having a corpse on your conscience, I've been thinking about Desmond."

"You have? When?"

"When you were getting dressed. You took ages. Anyway, my mind wandered back to the cave. You saw me die. And I actually accepted the fact I was going to die before that rock hit my head. I was completely helpless. There was poison in my blood. I couldn't move my arms or legs, I could barely speak. I thought there was a possibility we would survive, that we might somehow reset to a new timeline, but that was in no way a given. And I still accepted it. I threw myself at Captain Neville knowing it might be my last act in this life, and I was content. Because it was for the greater good. My death was preventing something very bad from happening to the world.

"I think, if he had been given the choice, Desmond would have accepted it as well. He wasn't able to voice his opinion, but I knew him. I knew his courage and selflessness. I believe if there's an afterlife, if he's looking down on us and telling me to stop blaming myself for what happened." She realized she was crying but she didn't want to draw attention to it by wiping at her cheek. "I thought I'd found peace before we left, but I don't think I truly had it until just now."

"This is also the second time since we've started working together that you've come within kissing distance of death."

"Third," Dorothy said.

"The necropolis, and..."

Dorothy said, "Fighting the Minotaur. It all worked out well in the end, but I had no illusions of surviving that encounter."

"Ah. Well, I'm referring to actual loss of consciousness and employing extreme measures to bring you back to health."

"Fine. I've only been on Death's door twice. Happy now?"

"Yes." Trafalgar kissed Dorothy's hair. "For what it's worth, I wholly believe you're correct about his point of view. And from what we've learned on this mission, there's almost certainly a timeline where Desmond lived. We could go back to the cave, skip back in time..."

Dorothy swatted Trafalgar's hand. "Don't even joke! I think we've done quite enough toying with the past for one week."

"Agreed."

They walked along down the main drag of town, no destination in mind. They passed a shop and Dorothy glanced inside, almost stopping dead in her tracks when she saw Rute inside.

The other woman was buying melons. She felt eyes on her and looked out the window, but her gaze slipped right over Dorothy when scanning for the threat. Trafalgar kept walking and Dorothy was pulled along by her until Rute was out of sight. Dorothy faced forward, as shaken as if she had just seen a ghost. The lack of recognition implied the other members of their party didn't necessarily recall the other timelines. That was definitely a good thing.

"Everything all right?" Trafalgar asked.

Dorothy smiled and patted Trafalgar's hand. "Just eager to get home, that's all. It's been a very long trip."

CHAPTER TWENTY-TWO

LONDON FELT stunningly urban after their stint in the jungle, although Dorothy still recalled spending a relatively relaxing few days in the bustling streets of Belém. Their long trip home had helped her arrange the conflicting accounts in a way that she hoped would prevent her from being confused in the future. Her time in the jungle, cutting through vines and swatting at mosquitos, was no less real to her than what she now accepted as reality. Though her "town" memories, as she'd come to call them, had become stronger and more vivid with time, the "jungle" memories remained just as clear.

"I suppose I will be stuck with the conflict," Dorothy said. She and Trafalgar were lying in bed together, not long after waking and on the verge of finally getting up in search of breakfast. "I shall always be able to remember two contrary versions of events for the same trip. It's odd, but it will be manageable."

"One of the many outlandish things we've filed away for the sake of our continued sanity," Trafalgar said.

She'd also spent much of their voyage considering the nature of memories. How strong was the mind, at the end of the day? The days training with her grandmother were vague, but she could still picture the older woman well enough to paint a portrait of her. But events from just a few years earlier were dim, as if all the colors had been drained out of them.

"All of our memories are redrawn every time we visit them," Trafalgar posited on their final day at sea. "Each time we go back, the actual memory changes just a little. It becomes vague, or we forget something. Eventually we're not remembering the actual experience, but the memory we created of it."

Dorothy said, "That's a bit frightening. Think of how easy it would be to 'remember' something that never actually occurred."

"That's why it's so dangerous to spend this life alone. Friends and lovers help remind us what is true."

Dorothy had smiled at that. "Loneliness... now *that* is something I doubt I'll ever have to worry about in this life. I have an abundance of people in my life."

Now, though, back on solid ground and in familiar territory, Dorothy was terrified that she was about to lose one of those people. Trafalgar suggested it would be best not to be present when Dorothy and Beatrice reunited. "Until we know for certain how she'll react... I don't wish to be the recipient of a warm welcome that is immediately regretted."

Instead, she summoned a cab which would take her to check on Cora Hyde. They'd had the benefit of "waking up" still in Brazil, but to go from the Pratear cave all the way back to London must have been utterly disorienting. There was also the danger that Cora may not know if her dueling memories were true or not. Trafalgar could, at the very least, confirm that she wasn't going insane.

Dorothy hesitated on the front steps of her home, envying Trafalgar's errand. At least she would be delivering good and comforting news. Her relationship with Beatrice had always been free and open. But perhaps it had been an unspoken rule that true feelings would never enter into her dalliances, that she would never carry on with a lover after the mission ended. She finally summoned the courage to open the door and step inside.

"Beatrice?"

She appeared on the second-floor landing so quickly that she must have been in motion before Dorothy spoke, probably from the moment she'd heard the door open. She wore her uniform shirt, suspenders, and slacks, but the shirt was untucked and her feet were bare as she hurried down the stairs with an enormous smile on her face. Dorothy felt a swell of love, almost brought to tears by the sight of the woman she loved being so comfortable in her... in *their* home.

"It's about time you got home, Lady Boone." Beatrice threw her arms around Dorothy in a hug, then pulled back to greet her properly with a long and slow kiss. "I've missed you, love."

Dorothy put her hands on Beatrice's sides, just above the waistband of her slacks. "I've missed you as well, Trix. Kiss me again."

"If I must."

Dorothy closed her eyes, brow furrowed. Every time she kissed Trafalgar, a part of her had twisted as if it was a betrayal of Beatrice. Now, with Beatrice's arms around her, she felt the reverse. She hated herself for betraying them both and, with great effort, pushed Beatrice away.

"There's something I have to tell you."

Beatrice's joy turned to concern. Her eyes darted across the exposed parts of Dorothy's body in search of scars or bandages.

"Are you all right? Were you hurt?"

"I'm... well, I was hurt, but I'm completely fine now. It's a very long story and it's not what we need to talk about." She lowered her head, unable to meet Beatrice's gaze for what she was about to say. "I don't know how to tell you this, Beatrice."

"You can tell me anything, Dorothy." She cupped Dorothy's cheek. "Please, just tell me."

Dorothy steadied her breathing but could do nothing to calm her heart. "Trafalgar and I... on the mission, there was... god, it's a long story, but... we slept together."

Beatrice dipped her chin and raised an eyebrow. "You and Trafalgar?"

"Yes."

"Okay." She tucked a hair behind Dorothy's ear.

Dorothy finally found the strength to look at Beatrice. "We were intimate several times in Brazil, and we continued on the trip home. I don't... know if we intend to continue now that we're home. But I also know that I don't wish to stop. I have feelings for her. She has feelings for me. And when we're together, it feels... it's..."

Beatrice's jaw was trembling. "Do you... wish to stop... w-with me?"

"No. God, no. If I was that callous, it would be simple. I may have feelings for Trafalgar, but I have no idea what they are. I *know* that I love you, Trix. I feel so selfish saying these things. I know how it must sound." She squeezed Beatrice's fingers. "I can walk away from her. She and I can go back to the way things were before we went to Brazil."

"Stop," Beatrice said. "I don't care."

Dorothy waited silently, watching Beatrice work through what she wanted to say. When she finally spoke again, her words were halting and quiet.

"Marriage... is... the most unappealing thing in the world to me. I see people with their wedding bands and I think that a shackle is no less confining because it happens to be forged from gold. I believe it's a strange sort of madness to ask another person to love you before all others for eternity. It's a contract and a vow for something which should be given freely every day. You slept with Trafalgar. And you care for her. And it's causing you so much pain right now. What good is that?"

Dorothy closed her eyes and felt tears on the lashes. Beatrice cupped her cheeks with both hands, and the tears fell free, rolling over her fingers.

"Say how you feel about me."

"Beatrice Sek, I love you," Dorothy said.

Beatrice kissed her lips. "I love you, too, Dorothy Boone. Trafalgar is a wonderful woman. I care for her myself. I'm not surprised by the idea you would eventually share a bed. I'm not surprised you would be reluctant to go back to just being colleagues after taking that step. I've always been willing to share you, because I know you will always come back to me. The only difference now is that you're being shared with someone who is sticking around."

"And you're honestly okay with that?"

"It may take a while to adjust," Beatrice admitted. "And I would hope she'll allow you to spend the night with me tonight, because I have missed you so terribly." She smoothed the collar of Dorothy's coat. "We may have to revisit this once we've had a chance to live with it for a while, just to confirm the theoretical lives up to the reality. My life is tied to yours, Dorothy. Whether you're only sleeping with me, or if you're sleeping with me and half the Mnemosyne Society. As long as you have a place in your heart for me, I will guard it with my life."

Dorothy kissed Beatrice's lips, then her cheek. "Beatrice," she whispered. "My Trix... you are the best thief I have ever encountered."

"How so?"

Dorothy pulled back and ran her hands through Beatrice's thick, dark hair. "You broke into my house with the intention of stealing only what you could carry. And now I'm standing here willing to give you everything I own. I'm sorry I can't offer you my entire heart."

Beatrice flattened her hand on Dorothy's chest. "I'm content to take only the part I can carry."

Dorothy pulled Beatrice to her, kissing her before guiding her upstairs.

Trafalgar had only visited Cora's house once. Dorothy wanted to check in when she returned from her stay at Wraysbury. On that visit, the curtains had been tightly drawn and the mood of her parlor lived up to its name. It had been a house in mourning. Now, however, every window was open wide to let in the early afternoon sunlight, and Cora greeted her with a smile which put that brightness to shame. She hugged Trafalgar hard enough to hurt, which made them both laugh. She was dressed in a pale blue blouse which accentuated the color of her eyes, and her dark hair was pinned back to expose her face. Trafalgar had never known her before the tragedy, so she'd had no idea how heavily it weighed on her appearance. She was seeing Cora's true smile for the very first time, unmarred by haunted eyes, and it was a beautiful sight.

"I knew you would be bald," Cora said when she finally let her go. She gripped Trafalgar by the upper arms and squeezed occasionally as if trying to confirm she was real. "If what happened was a dream or a hallucination, I wouldn't have known that. But I did. You look smashing, by the way. Did I say that before? Simply marvelous."

Cora served them both tea and explained her version of the past few weeks. "I remember the ocean journey as well as any I've ever taken. But I was also here. I had dinner with the Keepings. And yet, at the same time, I nearly died in the jungle with the two of you." She shook her head in amazement. "How do you and Dorothy recall everything?"

Trafalgar explained the conclusions she and Dorothy had come to, their conflicting accounts of parallel timelines and the days they spent with two versions of Felix Neville.

"I was ill," Trafalgar said, "and you took very good care of me. Even if that didn't actually happen in this timeline, I want you to know how grateful I am."

"It was my honor. And I believe it did happen. All of it. And not just because those experiences helped me overcome my mental strife, but because it feels more real than anything that happened here. We lived those days. And then, by setting things right, we forced the universe to manufacture a separate version of events. Think about it... the days you spent in Brazil. Did you do anything particularly out of the ordinary?"

Trafalgar thought. "We went sightseeing. We tried to convince Captain Neville to come home."

"But what did you see? Who did you meet?"

At the moment, she couldn't think of anyone in particular. "There were, ah, shopkeepers. Hotel staff." She tried to think of specifics. "There wasn't much of note, really."

"And my days here were mundane. I read books. I had dinner with old friends. I went to the same shops, I slept in the same bed. But the *other* timeline, the one where we discovered the Pratear... that is full of unique and singular events, new people. You must have done things in that timeline you've never done before."

"Dorothy..."

"Pardon?"

"I... Dorothy and I were, ah... intimate."

Cora sat up straighter, her eyes widening. "You what? When!"

"In the caves."

"Well, I never." She leaned forward and arched an eyebrow. "How was it?"

Trafalgar said, "It was private."

Cora rolled her eyes. "You're no fun. But it proves my point. That was the real timeline. That was everything that really happened, even the bad parts. You and Dorothy fixed things and this timeline was created to take its place."

"I like that version." Trafalgar reached out and put her hand on Cora's. "If for no other reason than it gave you closure on what's been haunting you."

"I don't think I'm completely myself yet. But the experience healed wounds I didn't even realize I had, so I'm confident that I'm on the road to recovery."

Trafalgar squeezed Cora's fingers. "That's magnificent. You deserve some peace."

"Thank you." Cora lifted Trafalgar's hand to kiss it. "Now, I'm sure your manners are telling you to stay and be sociable, but I'm sure you want to go home and rest after your trip."

"I'd be more than happy to stay for a while if you wish."

Cora shook her head. "For too long, I've been crowded by guilt and regret. Now those guests have finally fled, I'd like to spend some time getting reacquainted with myself."

"Solitude as self-exploration. I know the feeling." She stood and bent down to kiss Cora's cheek. "Be well, Cora Hyde. And when you're ready, I'm positive Dorothy will want to have you over to Threadneedle for dinner."

"I would enjoy that very much." She arched an eyebrow and smiled coyly. "Perhaps she will be more forthcoming with details of your new 'intimacy.'"

Trafalgar groaned, shoulders sagging. "Oh, good lord, she probably will be..."

Cora laughed and escorted Trafalgar to the door, offering her another bone-bruising hug before allowing her to leave. Trafalgar decided against taking a cab back to the townhouse so she could enjoy the fresh air, but also to give Dorothy and Beatrice more time alone. She had no idea what sort of conversation they might be having, but she did know that walking in on the middle of it would most likely not help any of them.

When she arrived, she found their luggage from the ship had already been delivered and was stacked at the base of the stairs. She paused next to the pile of bags and listened for sounds of distress or anger, but the house seemed curiously silent. The sitting room and parlor were empty, as was the kitchen at the back of the house, so she ventured higher. It wasn't until she reached the second landing that she heard signs of life coming from Dorothy's bedroom.

Trafalgar went to the door and held her breath. She thought she heard a sob, followed by the soft murmur of Beatrice's voice. A moment later she heard Dorothy respond at equal volume, but it was possible to hear what was said: "Beatrice." This was followed by another murmur and then Dorothy said it again, louder, "Beatrice!"

Trafalgar smiled and stepped away from the door, retreating as silently as she could so as not to disturb them. She stopped in her bedroom long enough to take off her shoes and exchange her traveling outfit for a more comfortable blouse and slacks, then went down to the kitchen to make herself a snack. There were days when she missed the home where she'd lived before joining forces with Dorothy, but the townhouse on Threadneedle had become special to her. There was something unique about it, cozy and powerful at the same time. She could almost feel the security of being surrounded by banks, as well as the extra precautions

Dorothy had put on her personal vault.

In the kitchen, she found the tea cookies and nibbled on them as she read the newspaper to catch up on what had been happening in their absence. She wondered if mundane events in London had been affected by what happened in the Pratear cave. In one version of the world, Cora Hyde was in Brazil. In this version, she was in London. Could the presence of one person cause enough of an effect to create a noticeable change in a city so large?

She was pondering this when she became aware of someone behind her. She turned and saw Beatrice, wearing a long shirt and baggy pants, lingering in the doorway of the kitchen. Her hair was mussed from her time in Dorothy's bed. The suspicion lifted from her features and she proceeded into the room, placing a hand on Trafalgar's shoulder as she passed.

"Dorothy neglected to mention you changed your look."

"I assume you had other topics to discuss."

Beatrice chuckled softly. She poured herself a glass of water and carried it back to the table. She snatched a few tea cookies before she sat down.

"It looks good. It suits you."

"Thank you." She stared at the newsprint to avoid meeting Beatrice's gaze. "I... assume the two of you did talk about the other change that occurred on this mission."

Beatrice said, "It was the first thing she said."

Trafalgar nodded and waited.

"Dorothy Boone," Beatrice said under her breath. "She's never been... She's... She has never been one to bind herself with tradition."

"No, no. Definitely not."

"It's one of the things I love most about her. I never wanted to restrict her. I never wanted to say she could only get satisfaction from me and me alone. The idea of Dorothy only having one lover for the rest of her life is as ludicrous as imagining her becoming a housewife and mother." They both laughed at that mental image. "She doesn't settle. Nothing, no matter how remarkable, holds her interest for very long. There's always something in the corner of her eye, stealing her attention. I held her attention for a very, very long time."

Her voice broke on the last word, and she covered it by taking a bite of the cookie. She chewed slowly and swallowed before she went on.

"I've always known that I would be sharing Dorothy. That's something you'll have to accept before you enter into any kind of romantic relationship with her. She loves with all her heart, but it's not a complete love. It never will be. The most you can hope for is that when she looks away, she'll eventually look back." Beatrice smiled and blinked rapidly. "She looked away and saw you. But she looked back at me. She got home, and... she still looked at me. I know she won't leave me behind, no matter what the two of you share."

"I won't allow her to," Trafalgar said. "I believe what the two of you share is too precious to be ruined by what we have."

"For now," Beatrice said. "In time, who knows?"

She finished her cookie, wiped the crumbs from her lips, and stood up. She paused next to Trafalgar's chair and bent down to place a soft kiss to the top of her head.

"I'm going to get dressed. And then I will go for a long walk. Dorothy is in her bedroom. I know you're probably exhausted from the trip, and I'm sure she wouldn't mind the company."

"Are you certain?" Trafalgar asked.

Beatrice squeezed Trafalgar's shoulder. "When I get back, I'll make dinner. Or I'll bring something. And the two of you can regale me with everything that happened in Brazil. I'm sure it's going to be quite a story. But for now, yes, I'm very certain that you should go upstairs and be with her."

"Thank you."

Beatrice patted Trafalgar's shoulder and went back upstairs. Trafalgar followed her up and slipped quietly into Dorothy's room. She pressed her back against the door and stared. Dorothy's room was opulent and lavish in a way that no other part of her life was. She had a four-poster bed complete with ruffled lace curtains, which were currently tied back. The furniture was antique and fragile. A few of Dorothy's outfits, which fit her like armor, were draped like tissue paper over the back of a chair. Heavy curtains had been drawn, probably by Beatrice, to keep the sunlight from disturbing her sleep.

And then there was the body lying in bed, impossibly small for the spirit it contained. Dorothy was more still and silent than Trafalgar was used to seeing her. A wave of red hair swirled above her head on the pillow, tangled curls like a small storm. Trafalgar moved closer to the bed and smiled down at the peaceful features of her friend. After a moment, there was a twitch behind the closed eyelids.

"Beatrice...?"

"It's me," Trafalgar said.

Dorothy pulled her hand out from beneath the pillow and held it out. "Get into bed with me, please."

Trafalgar did as requested. Dorothy made room for her, and they lay under the blankets facing each other. Dorothy scooted closer, and Trafalgar realized that Dorothy's habit of collecting lovers was far more than simple promiscuity. Dorothy Boone was the sort of person who loathed being alone. For all of her independence and self-reliance, in unguarded moments like this, she craved the weight of another body next to hers.

"I'm here, Dorothy," she whispered, honored to play such an important role in Dorothy's life. She put her arms around Dorothy's waist, cradled her head, and held her as she fell back to sleep.

EPILOGUE

A WEEK after their return from Brazil, Dorothy treated Trafalgar and Beatrice to afternoon tea at Café Royal. Dorothy wore a tweed suit, while Trafalgar chose an understated purple suit jacket over a skirt. She also wore a Musketeer hat to conceal her baldness. She normally didn't mind the stares her look attracted but, on this day, she felt they would draw enough attention being three unchaperoned women. Beatrice was the least comfortable of the trio. The only clothes she had nice enough for the restaurant were her work clothes, and Dorothy had made it clear they would not be acceptable. Beatrice was not there as a majordomo.

"You are a guest, the same as us, and shall be treated as such."

So she borrowed an outfit from Agnes Keeping which was appropriately classy but just a bit out-of-date. She kept touching her collar, the lapel, the cuffs, and kept her eyes forward so she wouldn't see if anyone was looking at her. Dorothy slipped an arm around her elbow and tried to reassure her that anyone who stared was merely jealous.

"Of me, or of my company?"

"Both are exquisite, darling," Dorothy said.

They were given a four-top table, choosing to have an extra place setting instead of deciding which of them would sit alone on one side of a booth. They were still perusing their menus when an Indian woman in a stunning red suit approached the empty chair. Dorothy recognized her immediately, but it took a moment for her to remember the woman's full name.

"Riya Lennox. Fancy seeing you here."

Riya smiled and dipped her chin in greeting. "Lady Boone, Miss Trafalgar, Madame Sek."

Beatrice blinked at the honorific, but said nothing.

"The Society was arranging a meeting to discuss your generous offer. We planned to meet in three days, on the weekend. I hope you're not here to inform us you've become impatient and wish to rescind the offer."

"No, not at all. In fact, I'm here to provide information which may help you come to a fully-formed decision. May I sit?"

Dorothy gestured. "By all means. We're all ears."

Riya pulled out the chair and sat. An attentive waiter bustled over, but Riya waved him off before he could begin speaking. Dorothy, Trafalgar, and Beatrice all closed their menus and focused on the woman positioned at what had just become the head of the table. She folded her hands on the napkin in front of her.

"I would ask how you're recovering from your recent mission to the Amazon, but there wasn't much in the way of physical damage on this trip. You both returned relatively unscathed."

Trafalgar looked at Dorothy, but both remained mum.

"Of course, that statement depends on which version of events you hear. There's the official report given to the Mnemosyne and Royal Geographical Societies. You spent a few days sightseeing and trying to convince Captain Neville to give up his quest. He was finally convinced by a dream of everything he stood to lose if he continued on his path."

"That's what happened," Dorothy said.

"Mm." Riya closed her eyes and began a recitation. "We engaged a tour guide by the name of Marco Eiriz to take us into the forest. This was the same man who had taken Felix Neville into the wilderness~"

Trafalgar slapped her hand on the table hard enough that people seated next to them jumped. Riya merely opened her eyes and looked at them again.

"Where did you get that?"

"Get what?" Dorothy asked.

"My journal," Trafalgar said, never looking away from Riya. "I wrote down my memories of what happened in case they began to fade. I haven't shown it to anyone. I don't intend to show it to anyone."

Riya said, "No, you haven't. And you won't for quite some time. You're quite elderly when you finally agree to let the journal be published." She withdrew a thin rectangular object from an inside jacket pocket and held her finger down on one corner. The face of the object lit up and she handed it to Trafalgar. She stared at the lit surface of the object, her face shining with its glow, and the anger in her expression gave way to confusion. She pressed her lips together and passed the object to Dorothy.

On the screen was what looked like a book's title leaf.

THE JOURNALS AND MEMOIRS
OF
TRAFALGAR OF ABYSSINIA
1920-1934
An Account of the Beginning of a Partnership with Lady Dorothy
Boone

Dorothy looked at Trafalgar, then at Riya. "Where did you get this?"

"Amazon," Riya said. "The bookseller, not the forest. It cost me about two pounds. Trust me, that's not as expensive as you might think. It's considered relatively cheap where I come from."

Beatrice had seen the screen now, and her hands were under the table. Dorothy knew she had filled them with weapons and Riya Lennox most likely had a gun aimed at her midsection. The shining device was sitting on the table and Riya picked it up, held down a button, and returned it to her suit jacket.

"Explanation," Dorothy said. "Now."

"The exact year of my birth isn't important but, suffice to say, you would consider it the future. I've been hearing stories about you for my entire life. My mothers were both fans of your exploits. Ma'am had a first-edition of that book. A physical copy. I spent so many years thumbing through it that I can still smell the leather of the cover." She finally looked at Trafalgar. "I can't express what an honor it is to sit at this table with you."

Trafalgar remained tight-lipped, silent.

"We wanted to contact you earlier, but we knew that even with your amazing lives it would be difficult to accept the idea of time travel. We had to wait until your experience with the Pratear so we would know for certain you would believe what we had to say."

Dorothy said, "You keep saying 'we'..."

The corners of Riya's lips twitched. She was obviously savoring what she was about to say. "By 'we,' I mean the Mnemosyne Society."

"I see." Dorothy's mind raced. "So you're from the future."

"Yes. We try not to travel back in time very often due to... well, you've seen the repercussions of messing with the time stream. There are too many potential pitfalls."

Trafalgar said, "But offering the Society twenty-five thousand pounds annually won't affect the time stream?"

"We offered the money because our mission has changed in recent years. We're less concerned with preservation of our own timeline if it means improving certain problems which have arisen."

"You want to use time travel to remake the world in your image."

Riya started to answer but then closed her mouth and thought a moment longer. "There has been much discussion about what you should be told about our intentions. Lady Boone, I told you that our deal was the annual stipend in exchange for accepting a mission from me at a later date."

"I remember."

"That mission will be to eliminate magic from the world."

Beatrice furrowed her brow. "You can't be serious."

"The survival of the world depends upon it. Last century, magic existed in small amounts all over the world. But during the Great War, it was tapped by more people in higher concentrations than ever before. It opened the door to a flood you're only beginning to see the effects from. These past few years, you've witnessed things you never would have dreamed possible." She looked at Beatrice. "And you, for instance. Discovering what you are~"

Dorothy snapped, "You will speak to her as a person."

Riya blinked in surprise. "I'm sorry?"

"'What' she really is," Trafalgar said. "You meant 'who.'"

"Oh. Yes, I'm... I'm sorry. I meant no disrespect to you, Madame Sek." She was obviously flustered by her mistake. She wet her lips and continued. "Magic has become a virus in the era I hail from. There have been great strides in technology and science, as you can see from the device I just showed you, but most people prefer the shortcuts allowed by magic. It took us too long to realize the consequences of what we were doing."

Dorothy said, "And what exactly might those be?"

"Magic is a part of this world's structure. Time and reality exist in a balance even our greatest minds don't understand. The Great War began an era of reckless magic use which strengthened some elements and weakened others. The walls began to crumble, just like they did in the Pratear cavern. The only reason we found a way to travel in time is because of fissures like the one you prevented. We're asking you to do the same thing you did in the cave, but on a much larger scale.

"One hundred years from now, humanity will be utterly dependent upon magic. Everyone will be adept. You would use it to butter your toast, to prepare your meal. And not long after that, it just stops. It's treated like losing a limb. No one remembers how to function on their own, how to survive without the shortcuts. Younger people are from a generation who never experienced a world without magic. We don't know if there's simply a finite supply of magic in the world or if it was the abuses which caused it to fade, but we do know the loss is catastrophic. It's called the Eschaton."

"The end of the world," Trafalgar said.

"It's how many people react to it, yes. Magic vanishes and society is thrown into chaos."

"But you want us to eliminate magic now," Dorothy said.

Riya nodded. "Now, when it would do the least amount of harm. Before it becomes a scourge. If magic went away now, it would be inconvenient but the world would continue as it did before the War. There might even be a place for it, a niche where it could continue to thrive without spreading to the entire populace. The only thing I know for certain is that the future depends on what happens here, now. And I believe you're the women for the job."

Dorothy said, "It's a big ask."

"And not something I want you to answer without full consideration." She pushed her chair back and stood. "I'll give you time. You may discuss it with the other members of the Mnemosyne Society. I'll return in a few days. If you choose to accept the deal, I will make arrangements for the first payment to be deposited in your accounts as soon as possible. Good day, ladies."

Beatrice waited until Riya was almost out of the restaurant before she stood up as well.

"Be careful," Dorothy said.

Beatrice brushed her hand across Dorothy's shoulders as she passed behind her, already focused on her target.

"What do you think?" Dorothy asked, once they were alone.

Trafalgar said, "I think it's plausible. Given everything we've seen and experienced. She had my journal. And we can't deny that the past few years have been, ah, odd."

"Are you talking about the Minotaur, or the time I spent with an ancient pharaoh living in my body?"

Trafalgar smirked. "Take your choice. If she's lying in an attempt to make us turn against magic for whatever reason, going along with her plan could be dangerous. There are portions of society which believe using magic is consorting with the Devil. She could be one of them with an unusually elaborate scheme."

Dorothy nodded. "Or... she could be telling the truth. She did know about the Pratear, and she had your journal."

"That device." Trafalgar shook her head in wonder. "It was all I could do not to stab her hand with a fork and run from the room with it. 1934. Over a decade of my own writing."

"If it was authentic."

"Yes, of course. If."

They sat silently. After a moment, Dorothy picked up her water glass and extended it toward Trafalgar.

"We'll discuss this with the Society later. For now, let us enjoy our afternoon tea in celebration of a successful mission."

Trafalgar tapped her glass against Dorothy's. "Hear, hear. Besides, if what we just learned is true, time is something we have in abundance."

"Indeed. I look forward to learning how we fill those years."

Dorothy winked and took a sip of her water, then turned back to the menu. Beatrice would return soon, and her report would hopefully give them a better idea as to whether or not they could trust Riya Lennox. They would enjoy their tea, and eventually they would bring up the matter of time travel and overreliance on magic to the Society. But all of that was for later.

She wasn't going to rush into anything, and she wasn't going to let a lovely afternoon go to waste on idle speculation.

For the moment, she had much more important matters on which to focus.

TRAFALGAR & BOONE

WILL RETURN IN

TRAFALGAR & BOONE

AGAINST

THE FORTY ELEPHANTS

ABOUT THE AUTHOR

Geonn Cannon lives in Oklahoma. He is the author of several novels, including the Riley Parra series which is currently being produced as a webseries for Tello Films, and an official Stargate SG-1 tie-in novel. Information about his other novels and an archive of free stories can be found online at geonncannon.com.

"Riley Parra is a strong, badass heroine for those that like their coffee and their cop fiction bitter." - P Industry

No Man's Land isn't the kind of place you go after dark, even if you have a badge. But Detective Riley Parra was born there, and she refuses to surrender it to the drug dealers, killers and criminals who have made it there home. The case of a body stuffed into a drainage pipe leads her to discover that there is far more at stake than she ever imagined.

~ **Riley Parra, Season One**.

"A good novel to while away a few hours in front of the fire." - Kitty Kat Reviews

Three years ago, Sofia Kennedy reported the tragic death of her girlfriend live-on air. Still in the closet even with her closest friends, she was forced to suffer her loss in silence. In the years since she's become isolated and sticks strictly to a routine that prevents her from encountering painful memories of the woman she lost.

Marion Vogt runs a small but well-respected catering service that feeds the elite of Seattle. When Sofia's consumer reporting segment does a story on Marion's company, the two women immediately butt heads. An unintended insult results in a scathing report that nearly shuts down the business. Marion's attempt to defend herself results in a deepening of their conflict until both women are ready to destroy one another.

They quickly find out Seattle can be a very small town when trying to avoid someone. As much as they want to avoid each other, fate keeps forcing Sofia and Marion to cross paths. Before long they realize they'll have to decide if they're going to hold on to bad feelings or risk forgiveness to discover just what they have to offer each other.

~ **Breaking Anchor**